WED TO THE
GRENDEL

Cara Wylde was born in Romania and grew up reading fantasy novels. She later transitioned to urban fantasy and paranormal romance, maybe earlier than it was age appropriate. But don't tell her mother! She now writes paranormal romance, science fiction romance, and reverse harem.

Arranged Monster Mates is a series she writes with Layla Fae and Eden Ember. These novellas follow different couples, are complete standalone stories, and can be read and enjoyed in any order.

carawylde.com

Wed to the Grendel

Arranged Monster Mates

First Digital Edition April 2024

Copyright © Cara Wylde 2024

All rights reserved.

No part of this publication may be reproduced, stored in a retrieval system, or transmitted, in any form or by any means, electronic, mechanical, photocopying, recording or otherwise without written permission from the author, except for the use of brief quotations in a book review.

This book is a work of fiction. The names, characters, places, and incidents are fictitious or have been used fictitiously, and are not to be construed as real in any way. Any resemblance to persons, living or dead, actual events, locales, or organizations is entirely coincidental.

WED TO THE GRENDEL

CARA WYLDE

ALIA TERRA

No one remembers the world before the Shift. It was thousands of years ago, all lost, all forgotten. Scientists and historians say that before, the world was better, brighter, and our planet belonged to us, humans. There were proud countries and bustling cities, and technology was at its highest.

We can hardly imagine all that. There is no proof, no written texts, no pictures of Alia Terra before the Shift. All we know is the face of Alia Terra now. The land haphazardly divided into territories, the walled cities, the poor living on the fringes, barely surviving.

The monsters.

The temples where young virgins can take a DNA test and be matched to one of them. An arranged marriage to a monster is often the only way a woman can save herself or give her family a chance to not starve.

This is Alia Terra. It belongs to the monsters, and we belong to them.

Branthor

The first day of spring. The mountain peaks were covered in thick snow that glowed in the sun, and the vale was lush green under the cloudless sky. Such a beautiful day had to be celebrated, and what better way to do that than to spend it with family?

"Branthor, is the meat ready?" my brother, Orion, yelled from the backyard.

"One minute," I yelled back as I added a fistful of crushed herbs to the thick slices of boar meat I'd just cut and laid out on the table before me. "This is art. It needs time."

My brother grumbled something, then I heard him and my two other brothers, Kairos and Ragnar, laugh. I shook my head and minded my own business. Lately, they had been talking behind my back, laughing and making jokes, and it was always something about how I was lonely and needed a wife.

In fact, I was not lonely. I was perfectly fine on my own, and I did not need a wife.

I had eyes. I could see how hard it was for Orion and his wife, Maren, with their two daughters, and Ragnar and Nova weren't doing any better with their son, Maverick, whose personality was true to his name. Now Kairos and Holly had a little one on the way, and soon, they would have to kiss their good night's sleep goodbye.

I, Branthor, the youngest of the four brothers, was the only one who could sleep when I wanted to, work when I felt like it, not work when I didn't feel like it, and not worry that the laundry basket was full, and the dishes had formed a wobbly tower in the sink.

I was living the life, and I very much wanted it to stay that way. No, I wasn't lonely one bit, thank you very much. At this point, I was starting to think my brothers wanted me to get a wife and start a family so I would be sleep-deprived like them.

I rubbed the herbs into the boar meat, transferred it onto a large plate, then washed my hands in the sink. Holly came in through the door that led to the back porch.

"Do you need help?" she asked, reaching for the plate I'd just loaded.

"No, no." I hurried to take it before she tried to. "I got it."

She smiled at me, her hands going to her round belly. I stepped outside, where my brothers were waiting and drinking ale. The fire for the barbecue was slowly turning to embers. I joined them, and we started placing the meat on the grill. Meanwhile, Holly joined Nova and Maren, who were chopping vegetables for a huge salad. Watching her, I shook my head and thought to myself, *"What was she thinking? She couldn't have lifted the plate all by herself."*

Sometimes, it was as if the three women – Holly, Nova, and Maren – forgot they were small, fragile humans married to literal giants. My brothers and I were grendels. The humans called us forest giants, but we called ourselves grendels, after the ancestor who was thought to have been the first of our race. We were twice as tall as the males of the human species. So, if the average height of a human male was 5 feet seven, then the average height of a grendel was 11 feet.

Mating between grendels and humans should have been impossible, but in this day and age, there were ways. Which was a good thing, because without human females, our race would've gone extinct by now. After the Shift, for reasons unexplained, very few female grendels were born, leaving the males without mates. The Marriage Temples that opened all over Alia Terra saved us. In exchange for a fee, they could find us mates among the humans. It wasn't ideal, but it was something.

Why wasn't it ideal? Because humans were tiny, which made it difficult for the females to carry a pregnancy with a grendel to term, not to mention that birthing a human-grendel hybrid was dangerous. The Marriage Temples came to our rescues and gave us medicine to help the women, so now, it was easier and safer than it used to be. However, there was another problem. The hybrid children didn't grow up to be as big and strong as the pure-blooded grendels, which in time had caused a divide between us.

My community was pro-mating with humans, but I knew of grendel communities that had chosen to isolate themselves. Some of them had a few females, but others were made up of celibate males only. It was a hard life with few rewards, so that was why I was glad my family belonged to the community of Mossdale. We lived high in the mountains, surrounded by forests, and we had our valley where we grew our food and our farm animals, and raised our hybrid children. Even though I was never going to take a mate and have offspring myself, I loved being surrounded by cheerful families.

Holly, Nova, and Maren were laughing and chatting loudly, and the little ones were playing in the playground Orion had built for his two girls, Pearl and Coral. Pearl was four years old, and her sister, Coral, was six. Because their cousin, Maverick, was only two, they looked after him. They were all young – very young, indeed – but because they were hybrid children, Pearl and Coral were already as tall as their mother, Maren. Maverick was getting there fast, and his mother, Nova, couldn't carry him anymore, even if he was only two, and basically a baby.

That was why grendel fathers needed to step up. A human mother could carry her baby in her arms for, maybe, ten or twelve months, and then the baby would grow to be too heavy for her. The father had to be on duty twenty-four seven, waking in the middle of the night to change diapers and rock the fussy baby to sleep.

I loved my nephew and two nieces. I thought they were perfect, and I was ready to die for them. Well, maybe not Maverick – he could be annoying, like his dad, Ragnar. However, I wasn't ready to be a father. I didn't think I was made for it, in fact, so I honestly didn't expect to ever be ready.

Kairos caught me watching the kids play and elbowed me in the ribs.

"When will it be your turn?"

"My turn for what?"

"To contribute to this growing family," he said, laughing.

Ragnar, who was flipping the meat on the grill, huffed and shook his head. "Do you know what our brother's problem is?"

Orion opened another bottle of ale and cocked an eyebrow. "What is it?"

"He's selfish," Ragnar said. "Too selfish to share his home, his food, and his life with someone else."

I rolled my eyes. I was so tired of this conversation.

"How can I be selfish?" I said. "Towards whom? A wife I don't have and children that don't exist?"

"Towards us," said Ragnar.

I sighed. "Make it make sense, brother."

Orion took over. "No, he's right. Here is the new generation." He pointed at Pearl and Coral, who were taking turns going on the slide while Maverick was cheering them on. "They need cousins, the more the better, so they can make Mossdale thrive when we won't be here anymore."

"There are plenty of kids their age in Mossdale," I said. "They don't necessarily need to be their cousins."

"Friends are good," said Kairos. "Family is better."

Mossdale was what we called our valley – our home. If I wasn't mistaken, we were around a hundred and fifty souls living here – pure-blood grendels, human wives, and hybrid children. The only female grendels in Mossdale were two old women, Sava and Varna, who lived together in a house by the river. They babysat for everyone in Mossdale, and twice a week, they taught history classes at our school.

I couldn't argue with my brothers. Family was the best. Our parents had passed away a long time ago. Since I was the youngest, I barely remembered them. Our mother passed soon after I was born, crushed that she was too old to try again and hopefully have a daughter. She and our father had tried four times, and four times, they had sons. She loved us, but she'd wanted a daughter so badly that it broke her heart, and eventually, she lay down one night and didn't wake up in the morning. Of course, I was aware she'd probably been sick, but our father had insisted she'd died of misery, and at some point, my brothers and I stopped contradicting him. He passed on a few years later, so we were left on our own. My brothers raised me, and Mossdale raised all of us.

"I wouldn't be a good husband," I said. "And I'd be a worse father."

"Why do you say that?" Kairos asked.

The meat was done, and Orion started loading two plates with it.

"Human females are tiny and frail," I said. "I wouldn't know how to take care of one. I wouldn't know how to be gentle, and patient, and kind."

Kairos shook his head. "I did notice you're avoiding Holly, Nova, and Maren at all costs."

"I'm not avoiding them!"

"As in, you avoid touching them. They're not that fragile, Branthor. You can touch Holly's belly and feel the baby kick, you know. She'd love it."

I cocked an eyebrow. "Did she tell you that?" The truth was, I thought Holly was the frailest of them all. She had yellow hair and pale skin, and if she as much as accidentally brushed her arm against a furniture corner, her skin immediately turned blue and purple.

Kairos shrugged. "Not in those exact words. I believe she said to me a few nights ago, 'Is Branthor scared of my belly?' And just this morning, she didn't want to come to the barbecue because, and I quote, 'Branthor can't even look at me. I bet he thinks I'm fat.' So, I'm just saying, brother. They're not that fragile, and you're insulting Holly, Nova, and Maren by avoiding them so fiercely."

"I had no idea! Holly is not fat! I would never think that!"

Kairos, Ragnar, and Orion burst out laughing, and for a second, I wondered if they were making fun of me. Surely, Holly knew I respected and admired her.

I just didn't think it was acceptable for me to put my big paw on her round belly, even is I was curious to meet the baby who was soon going to be born.

We let the embers die and took the grilled meat to the large table Orion and his wife, Maren, had set up in their backyard. We all lived close to each other, but when we gathered for a barbecue, it was usually at Orion's house. He had the biggest yard.

The table was laden with meat, freshly baked bread, colorful salads, and three massive cherry pies Nova and Maren had baked together. I sat down next to Holly, so she wouldn't think I was avoiding her. Ragnar sat down next to me, with Maverick on his lap.

Maverick, being Maverick, grabbed the knife and started waving it around. Ragnar cursed under his breath and quickly snatched it from his hand just as I was reaching for the bread. The knife sliced across my arm, and I winced and scrambled to stop the bleeding with a napkin.

"Branthor, are you okay?" Nova jumped from her highchair and rushed to my side. "Maverick, look what you did," she scolded her son.

"It's okay, Nova," I said. "It's just a scratch. I'll go wash it."

Ragnar scolded his son too, though he had been the one to nick me with the knife. He gave me his napkin to replace the one that was soaked with blood.

"Here. Keep the pressure on," he said. "Give me that." He took the dirty napkin as his wife rushed me inside the house.

"It's nothing," I told Nova. "Really, you shouldn't worry about me."

"Nonsense. I was a nurse in my previous life, so let me help you."

Indeed, before marrying my brother, Nova had been a nurse in one of the walled cities of the humans. She didn't like talking about her life before, so I didn't press her to tell me more. I let her bandage my wound, all the while thinking how lucky I was to have a family that cared.

Maybe that was why my brothers kept pestering me about finding myself a bride. Because they cared.

Teal

The bread was in the oven, but I had yet to chop the veggies and throw them in a pot with the chicken thighs for the stew. Had it been my choice, I would've opted for a lighter, easier dinner, but chicken stew had been the food order my father and two brothers had put in when they stopped by to have lunch a few hours before.

I was running late. All day, I'd been busy doing the laundry and the cleaning, and then, when I thought I was done and I could start on dinner, a pipe burst in the bathroom, and I had to deal with it to the best of my ability. Better to patch it up myself than have the men of the house come home to a small flood and say it was my fault.

I was good at repairing things around the house. I had to be. My father was a Peacemaker, and my older brothers had followed in his footsteps. The three of them were too busy to deal with home repairs, and when they finished their shift in the evening, they expected a warm dinner, a cold beer, and to be left alone to rot on the couch. If they had to lift a finger to help me with anything, they threw a tantrum. Sometimes they even threw a punch or two, for good measure, to teach me a lesson.

It had been this way since my mother passed away, a week before I turned eighteen. I would never forget her last words to me.

"Teal, the day you turn eighteen, send your blood to the Temple. Promise me, my love."

"An arranged marriage to a monster," I said. "Is that what you want for me?"

"I want you to be happy, cherished, and protected. The monsters are here, Teal, in this house, and I'm sorry I must leave you with them."

I promised her, and on my eighteenth birthday, I sent a sample of my blood to the Marriage Temple, in secret. It had been five years since then. I was twenty-three and still living in hell.

I chopped the onions so fast that I nicked my finger. I yelped, wrapped my finger in a paper napkin to stop the bleeding, then washed the tiny wound with cold water. I didn't have time to bandage it properly. I had to chop the garlic next, then the carrots, the potatoes, and the bell peppers. I checked the clock, let out a pathetic whimper, and moved faster, my hands shaking from anxiety. My father and my brothers would be home soon, in an hour – an hour and a half, if I was lucky – and dinner would have to be waiting for them on the table. They expected nothing less.

Not that I hadn't tried to run away. The first time I tried, it was soon after my mother's funeral. The day she was put into the ground, I dared to confront my father and give him a piece of my mind. Crying, I told him he'd killed her. He and his sons that he'd raised to be brutes, like him. With their demands, with their refusal to help around the house, with the endless labor they had created for her. They'd treated her like a slave, until she got sick and couldn't get out of the bed anymore, and they moved her to a tiny room with one small, square window, and pretended she was already dead.

My mother had done her best to protect me. I started helping her around the house since I could walk, but she made sure to do most of the work, so I could go to school, have time to do my homework and read books. She thought education was going to save me. Well, it didn't.

Then she was gone, and I was the slave who replaced her. When I was nineteen and had my first boyfriend, my brothers followed him home one night and beat him up so he would break up with me. Since then, boys my age knew to stay away from me. My brothers weren't going to allow anyone to take me away and save me from them. They needed me to do their laundry, fold their clothes, keep the house clean, and make their food.

The day of my mother's funeral was the first and last time I confronted my father. He slapped me so hard that I couldn't get out of the house for a week, afraid the neighbors might see my swollen eye. No one was going to help me. We lived in a neighborhood of Peacemakers, in one of the most prosperous walled cities in the state – Fortitude. My father and my brothers were respected and never questioned. No one cared about me. To be fair, the other Peacemakers' daughters and wives didn't have a much better life. Peacemakers were known to be brutal. They had to be to keep the peace. After seeing only violence at their job, it was hard to detach when they got home to their families.

Not that it was an excuse.

When I turned twenty-one, I couldn't take it anymore. I had no money, so I stole some from my dad, packed a small bag, and ran away. I didn't make it out of the city. The minute my dad realized I was gone, he alerted all the other Peacemakers, they dropped everything, and found me within an hour. Once back home, I had to endure more than a slap. I didn't walk out of the house for two weeks.

So here I was, at twenty-three, my life unchanged. I wasn't allowed to have my own money, was barely allowed out of the house, and only to get groceries, I had no friends, and wasn't allowed to be around men that weren't my dad or my brothers.

Here I was, finally dumping all the chopped veggies and the chicken in a pot, seasoning everything with salt and herbs, imagining it was poison.

No, I would never do such a thing. I wasn't like them. I didn't want to end their lives, I just wanted to be able to leave and never look back.

I took out the bread, let it rest for ten minutes, then cut thick slices. When the stew was ready, I poured generous portions into three bowls and set them on the table in the dining room just as the front door opened.

My heart was beating wildly in my chest even though I'd gotten everything ready before their arrival. But that was how it went. They'd get home every evening, and even though I'd spent the day making sure things were exactly as they liked, there was always a chance I'd missed something or gotten the tiniest detail wrong. I could control the work I did around the house and my behavior, but I couldn't control their tempers.

My father stomped into the dining room, followed by my two brothers. I instantly knew something wasn't right. Usually, they'd wash up and change first, then have dinner.

"Hi," I said, my voice small and weak. "How was work today?"

My father scowled while my brothers exchanged glances and shook their heads.

"Um... I made the stew that you like." I gestured at the table, hoping the steaming food would get their attention. They were angry with me, I could tell, but for the life of me, I couldn't say why. And I didn't dare to ask. My best bet was to distract them. "I started on some chocolate chip cookies. They'll be ready in half an hour." That was a lie. But I only needed five minutes to make the cookie dough, if only they let me retreat to the kitchen.

"Shut up." My father was seething. "Shut up, Teal. You've done it this time."

I took a step back and put a chair between me and him. "What do you mean? I didn't do anything."

"Then what is this?"

He took out a white envelope and threw it on the table. My eyes widened when I saw the sigil of the Marriage Temple. I knew it well. I'd been hoping to see it these past five years. I was in charge of the mail, but today I'd forgotten to get it, what with the burst pipe I'd had to patch up and the dinner I'd had to rush.

"Speak, Teal," he ordered me. "Have you gone mute?"

In fact, yes, I was suddenly mute. I didn't know what to say. My body started shaking, and I felt sick. I knew what was coming. In my head, I cursed the stupid pipe and my bad luck. I should've been the one to find the letter in our mail. Then I could've hidden it and gone straight to the Temple the next day, after they went to work. And when they realized I was missing and sent their Peacemaker friends after me, the letter would've stopped them from bringing me back home.

Because once the Marriage Temple found a match, no one could stop the mating ceremony from happening. Not even the Peacemakers.

My father slammed his fist on the table. I jumped and looked into his eyes, seeing only darkness.

My lips started moving, but I could barely make a sound. I cleared my throat and tried again.

"It was a long time ago. I didn't think I'd ever get a letter."

"You went over my head and sent your blood to the Temple," he said. He was so furious that every time he spoke, spit flew from his mouth. "My daughter! My only daughter wants to give herself to a monster! To a beast with... with a tail, and horns, and a forked tongue, or whatever the hell they have!"

"They're not all the same."

That only made him angrier. In two steps, he was in front of me, hand raised. I screamed and tried to cover my face, but he caught me right in the jaw. The pain was so terrible that tears spilled out of my eyes. He hit me again, and I retreated into a corner of the room, where I curled up with my knees to my chest and my back to him, trying to protect myself. My brothers didn't stop him. On the contrary, when our dad was done with me and stomped away, they came over and kicked me in the ribs, just to make it clear they weren't pleased, either.

I knew they couldn't do anything about the letter. They knew it, too. When I was finally alone in the room, I rushed and grabbed the envelope, then locked myself in my bedroom. I heard them move around the house, wash up in the bathroom, eat their dinner, then go out onto the porch to smoke and drink beer until late at night. They didn't knock on my door, didn't seek me out to talk to me or hit me again. This told me they'd accepted the situation. In their own way.

Tomorrow, I was going to be free at last. Under the covers, I read the letter over and over again. I didn't know who my mate was. Neither his name, nor his species were mentioned. I didn't care. Whoever he was, he was better than the monsters I'd lived with all my life. The monsters who'd sent my mother to an early grave.

Whoever he was, I was going to be a perfect wife to him. So he'd keep me. Far, far away from this hell.

Teal

I walked to the train station.

Early the next morning, my father and my brothers were waiting for me in the living room. At first, I thought they wanted me to fix them breakfast, but when I made to go into the kitchen, Dad stopped me.

"I want you out of the house," he said. "You're not my daughter anymore. You're a whore. Monster whore."

I grit my teeth and swallowed heavily. In my head, I kept repeating to myself, *"he's wrong, he's wrong, he's wrong"* and, *"don't believe him, don't believe him, don't believe him"*. I was not a whore. I was a desperate woman. No matter what he said, I didn't care. I would not listen to him. If he wanted me out of the house, good.

"I'll go get my things," I said.

"Your things? You don't have things."

"I mean, my clothes."

"You don't have clothes. Everything you have, I bought and own. Be grateful I'm letting you keep the clothes on your back."

I bit my tongue to stop myself from arguing with him. The labor I'd done for him and my brothers all these years meant nothing. Fine. As long as I could leave, I was okay with having only the clothes on my back. But how was I going to get to the Temple?

"Get out," my father said.

That was my cue. I wasn't going to wait to be told twice. My brothers didn't meet my eye as I went past them and out the front door. I didn't look back.

I walked to the train station. Once there, I needed money to board the train and no clue how to get it. Had I had any friends, I would've asked for a loan. Just a tiny loan, enough to buy myself a one-way ticket. The Marriage Temple was two cities away. For some reason, Fortitude had always been against the Temples. Not a lot of women who lived in Fortitude sent their blood to be matched to a monster. Years ago, before I was born, when there was a plan to build a Marriage Temple just outside the city walls, the locals stopped it. My mother had told me the story.

I felt lost in the crowded train station. I felt choked with anxiety, too, and it was hard to breathe. Because I was out of my father's house, but I was not out of the city. He could change his mind at any moment, come looking for me, and bring me back home, where he could do anything he wanted. What if it suddenly struck him that it was better for me to be dead than married to what he considered a monster?

I had to get out of Fortitude. I had to get out now.

Without allowing myself to think too much, I boarded the train. Without a ticket. What was the worst that could happen? If I was caught, I would get a fine. So what? Once I got to the Temple safely, and my arranged husband paid for the Temple's services, I could easily pay the fine.

I couldn't believe I was so panicked over getting on the train without a ticket or money to pay the fare. It was ridiculous. I felt ridiculous. I'd survived so much; I couldn't let this be an obstacle. So, I found a seat near the window and told myself I was going to be okay. My nightmare would be over soon. The train started moving, and I kept my eyes glued to the passing sights beyond the window. When the train finally rolled out of Fortitude, I allowed myself to release a deep, heavy breath.

Of course, ten minutes later, a man in uniform asked to see my ticket.

"I... I don't have a ticket, I'm sorry."

"You can buy one. Where are you traveling?"

"I don't have any money, I'm sorry." To answer his question, I showed him the letter from the Temple.

He looked at it, frowned, and gave it back. "I'm sorry, Miss, you still have to buy a ticket, or I'm afraid you'll have to get off at the next station."

At least he didn't mention anything about a fine. I bit the inside of my lip, trying to come up with something that would convince him. Though I knew he wasn't going to let himself be convinced. He was only doing his job, and these were the rules.

"I'll pay for her ticket," the lady sitting in front of me said, reaching into her purse.

My eyes widened. She was small and frail, with gray strands in her honey brown hair. She must've been in her fifties. When she looked at me and smiled, she reminded me of my mother. This was what my mother would've probably looked like in middle age, had she lived.

The man accepted the money, his little machine printed the ticket, and he gave it to me before moving on.

"Thank you so much. You saved me."

The lady waved me off. "Please, it's nothing. I have a daughter who found her match two years ago. I took her to the train station myself. I miss her every day, but I know she is happy."

"I'm glad she's happy. Maybe I will be, too."

She gave me another encouraging smile. "Trust that you will."

I arrived at the Temple at noon. I was hungry and cold. The weather had turned, it was now cloudy and chilly, and I was only in a dress. My father hadn't even allowed me to take a jacket with me. The Temple servants – two young, pretty girls – welcomed me and took me to a chamber where I could wash up and rest. They told me the room was mine. Attached to it, there was a small bathroom with a narrow tub.

"You won't be with us long, though," one of them said. "Your future husband will be here tomorrow."

That made me feel anxious and a little scared. What if he arrived tomorrow, saw me, and decided he didn't like me? As the girls went to fetch me something to eat – their words, not mine – I stepped into the bathroom and looked in the mirror.

I was small for my age. All the stress and sadness had eaten away at me, and I was pale, thin, too short, and too frail. I looked rather pathetic. Not like a confident woman, but like a lost little girl. When my mother was twenty-three, she'd already had my oldest brother and was pregnant with her second son. The sons who were going to be her undoing. I arrived a few years later, and unfortunately, didn't make her life easier.

I had her white-blonde hair and blue-green eyes. That was why she'd named me Teal. I missed her terribly, and even though staring at my reflection gave me anxiety about what my future husband was going to think, at least I could see her features on my face. I had her bone structure and her dark, straight eyebrows.

The servant girls brought me lunch.

"This is for your..." One of them passed me a small tube of medicine, gesturing at my face.

"Oh." I touched my jaw, where my father had hit me the night before. I was so used to being covered in bruises that I didn't notice them anymore. Now I thought back to the lady on the train and what she might've thought about me. I felt so embarrassed that I could die. "Thank you."

"It's an ointment made by the orcs. Their kind knows so much about plant medicine. It will help you heal quickly."

My eyes filled with tears. "I am so grateful for your help."

She smiled at me. The other servant girl, trying to change the subject, told me that I was free to explore the gardens, if I wanted to. Then they left me alone, and I could finally let the tears fall. When I felt a little better, I looked outside the window. It had started raining, and the truth was, all I wanted to do was eat and take a nap. Finally, I could sleep peacefully, and not worry I might've forgotten to do something around the house.

The day I spent at the Temple, and the night I slept in that cozy little room, were the best I'd had in my whole life. I never wanted to leave, but I knew I had to. I wasn't here on vacation; I'd come to meet my arranged husband and follow him wherever he would take me.

However, the next day, I was in for a surprise.

The Temple servants dressed me up, brushed my hair, and applied a little makeup to make me look... well... alive. I'd used the ointment on my face and body, where my father and my brothers had hit me. The bruises disappeared within a few hours, and it was nice to see that my skin was perfect again.

The girls told me I was expected in the great hall, where the priest was going to perform the ceremony. With my heart beating in my throat and my hands sweating profusely, I walked into the great hall. I was about to see my mate for the first time. I was about to finally find out who he was, what he looked like, and to what species he belonged.

Three people were waiting for me. In fact, two people, and one... giant. The priest, in his long, purple robes, was standing in front of the altar, a deep frown on his face. Before him, a woman with long, blonde hair that touched her waist, and a round belly she gingerly rested her hands upon, was shifting from one foot to another, most likely trying to ease the ache in her back. Next to her, a mountain of a man with coarse black hair and a long beard was standing awkwardly, not really knowing what to do with his clumsy limbs. He was so tall that the top of his head was only inches away from touching the ceiling.

I approached them warily. This giant couldn't be my mate. He and the woman seemed to be together. It was easy to guess from the looks he gave her. He seemed concerned for her well-being, but when he suggested she sat down, she shushed him and insisted she was fine.

"There she is," the woman said, spreading her arms wide and waddling over to me. "You must be Teal. What a beauty you are!" As she got closer, I saw her wince. "Some meat on your bones wouldn't hurt, but I reckon that can be easily fixed."

She stopped in front of me, unsure if she could hug me or not. She wanted to, but I had no idea who she was, so I didn't make any gesture that might've been interpreted as giving her permission.

"Hi," I said.

"Hi! I'm Holly. Your sister-in-law. Well, one of them. You have three sisters-in-law. Isn't it exciting? Me, Nova, and Maren."

I blinked at her, confused. On the one hand, that was great news. Wherever my new home was, I wasn't going to be alone. I guessed that since Holly was human, Nova and Maren were human, too. Sisters-in-law. Sisters. Oh, how easy my life would've been had I had sisters instead of brothers!

On the other hand, this was unexpected. Where was my husband?

"Hi," the giant said, waving at me. "I'm Kairos, Holly's mate. We've come to take you to your new home."

"Um... wasn't my mate supposed to come?" I asked.

At that, Holly clapped her hands and laughed. "The funny thing is..." Her laugh turned into a nervous chuckle. "It's funny, you're going to laugh..."

"This is highly unusual," the priest said, his voice rising above Holly's. "I don't feel comfortable with this arrangement, I must say."

"What arrangement?" I asked, my heart hammering in my chest.

"Holly and Kairos are here to sign the marriage contract that will bind you, Teal, to your mate, Branthor. I cannot perform the mating ceremony if your husband isn't present, and the signing of the contract is only half of the process. Not even half, since Branthor himself will not be signing, and his brother and sister-in-law will sign in his stead."

"Branthor will sign," Kairos said. "Do not worry, once we take his bride to him, he will sign, and I will personally make sure the Temple receives a copy of the signed contract."

This whole exchange was making me dizzy. What was happening? Why was my future husband not here? Did he, in fact, not want me?

"What does this mean?" I asked, unable to hide my concern. "If my mate isn't here for the ceremony, and if he doesn't sign the contract... Does it mean that if I go with them," I motioned at Holly and Kairos, "it doesn't mean anything? Because the marriage isn't set in stone, then my future... um... possible husband can change his mind?"

The priest looked at me and shrugged. His reaction didn't reassure me at all.

"No!" Holly reached for both my hands, and I allowed her to take them in hers. "No, no, no. That won't happen. Teal, you are perfect for Branthor. He will sign the contract, no questions asked."

"What questions might he ask?" This was just my luck.

"No questions," Holly said quickly.

"Wait. It sounds to me like Branthor doesn't even know about me. Doesn't know he was... matched."

Holly chuckled again, then turned to her husband, Kairos, for help. To look into his eyes, she had to crane her neck in an almost painful manner.

"My brother can be difficult," he said. "But that's why he has us, his family. When he can't see what's good for him, we do, and we take action."

Oh, gods! This did not sound good. It did not sound good at all!

Kairos turned to the priest. "I have the Temple fee right here. I can pay now, and I will sign wherever you need me to."

The priest sighed, but eventually nodded and motioned for him to approach a table with a silver platter on it, and a stack of papers that were waiting to be read and signed. Kairos dropped the coins on the platter, and while the priest counted them, signed on every page without reading a single word.

"I'm only allowing this because I have held the ceremonies that bound you to Holly, your brother Ragnar to Nova, and your brother Orion to Maren," the priest said. "I trust you. I know how much family means to you, and I know that Teal is in good hands. However, I will ask to send a Temple delegate to check on the bride within one week's time. We care about what we're doing here. We want it done right."

"Of course," Kairos said. "We will welcome the delegate with open arms. Let us know the day of the visit, and we will prepare a feast."

At least the priest was looking out for me.

"Teal," he said after he finished counting the credits and set an amount aside. "Do you wish for the credits to be sent to your family?"

"No!" My little outburst drew Holly's attention, and she looked at me with concern in her eyes. I cleared my throat. "No."

"The money is yours, then."

That left me speechless.

"Normally, a bride will want us to send it to her family, or a friend in need."

"I don't have friends. In need," I added belatedly.

This was unbelievable! I could keep the money?

"You could also donate it," he said.

Donate it to whom? To what? I'd lived in a bubble all my life, and I knew nothing about charities or organizations that helped the needy. Now I felt foolish and selfish. But maybe I could take the money and decide who to donate it to later. Or, I could take the money and keep it, just in case this Branthor that I had yet to meet didn't sign the marriage contract and sent me back to whence I came. And then I'd need the money to carve a life for myself away from my father and two brothers. Whatever happened next, one thing I knew for sure: I wasn't going to set foot in Fortitude ever again.

"I'll keep it," I said.

BRANTHOR

The days leading up to my sixtieth birthday were... odd, to say the least. Everyone was agitated, but in a strange, anxiety-inducing way. And everyone wanted me out of their way.

Holly, Nova, and Maren loved organizing birthdays. Not that grendels didn't celebrate birthdays, but the way humans did it was on another level. Gifts, a lot of food, even more alcohol, music, dancing, and fireworks were mandatory. Oh, and a huge birthday cake. Before we started mating with human females, my species had enjoyed something sweet here and there, but now that Mossdale was the home of so many human brides, it was as if it had turned into a cake factory! It was my personal opinion that humans could not live without sugar, and now that they'd introduced it to us, grendels were starting to see the appeal of it, too.

Still, did birthdays really warrant such humongous cakes? A few years ago, Maren had said her dream was to one day build a cake as big as her husband, Orion. Females and their ideas...

On the one hand, I was used to them doing this every year, and this year was special. A grendel turned sixty only once, right? I was young. My plan was to not worry about the future until I hit eighty. On the other hand, the atmosphere in the valley felt strange. Heavy. It seemed like everyone was involved somehow, not just my brothers and their families. They whispered among themselves, but the second they noticed I was around, they would go silent and wait for me to leave, or they would straight up shoo me. It felt more like a conspiracy than the preparation of a birthday surprise.

Then Holly and Kairos disappeared for a whole day, and that confused me even more. I noticed they used the portal, which we'd installed in a special building we'd made for it near the river. It was our only connection to the outside world. We were located too deep and high in the mountains, and it was nearly impossible to reach other people – humans or monsters – by car, carriage, or any other means of transportation. I wondered where my brother and his wife had gone. Maybe they needed to do some last-minute shopping. That was what I told myself, at least.

The night before my birthday, I barely slept. There was something in the air. I hadn't seen Holly and Kairos return to Mossdale, but when I asked Ragnar about them, he told me they were home. When I wanted to visit, he stopped me, saying that Holly wasn't feeling well. That worried me. Between the whole town acting weird and Holly possibly being ill, I was certain my birthday was going to be a disaster. Not that I cared. All I wanted was for everyone to go back to normal. They were making too big a deal out of a day whose sole purpose was to remind me I was getting old.

Morning couldn't come fast enough. At the crack of dawn, I jumped out of the bed, took a quick shower, then went straight to Ragnar's house. I knew he was up because his son, Maverick, rarely slept past five o'clock. Surely enough, I found him in the kitchen, rocking the toddler in his arms. Maverick was screaming at the top of his lungs, and Ragnar wasn't having much luck quieting him down.

"What happened?" I asked.

My brother rolled his eyes at me. "He broke his favorite toy, now he's shattered." At that, the boy screamed even louder. "You did it with your own two hands," Ragnar told him. Then, to me, "He's just discovering how strong he is. He'll learn to control it, but it will take a while."

"How can Nova sleep with all this ruckus?"

Ragnar laughed. "Oh, she's used to it. She's been working so hard these past few days. Her head hits the pillow and she's out."

Impressive. I would never stop being astonished by how resilient human females were.

"About that," I said. "What have you been working on? Orion and Kairos won't tell me a thing. I can't even convince Holly or Maren."

"Your birthday party, silly." He shook his head as he kept rocking Maverick, who was still not letting up. "Have a little patience."

"That's not it," I protested. "I'm not impatient."

"Then what are you doing here, trying to get information out of me?"

I huffed. "I'm not. I mean, I am. It all feels weird, okay? It feels like... you're plotting something."

"Yes. A birthday party. Like we do every year, for each of us."

"No, it feels like you're plotting something… something…" What was the word?

Ragnar raised his eyebrows at me.

"Nefarious!" Yes, that was the word.

One beat. Two beats. Then my brother started laughing so thunderously that I was certain there was no way his wife would sleep through that. Even Maverick stopped screaming, his big, dark eyes fixed on his father. Ragnar put him down so he could wipe the corners of his eyes.

"Oh, it's good to have a laugh early in the morning. Sets you up for a bright day."

I frowned. "I'm not joking, Ragnar. Something feels off, and I need you to tell me what's going on. What are you all up to? This isn't just a regular birthday party, and you know it."

"Seriously, brother, you're starting to sound paranoid."

He gave me a smirk, and I knew I was right. No matter what he said, they were planning something nefarious. My own brothers! Truth be told, I could expect anything from them.

"Go home," he said. And then, he actually started pushing me towards the front door. Once again, I was being shooed. "Relax. Don't think about it. It's a surprise, okay? A surprise is to be enjoyed fully when the time comes, not to be revealed in advance."

I was out the door, and Ragnar was about to shut it in my face.

"I'm not sure I'll like this surprise," I said.

"Nonsense. You like all our surprises." And "bang!" the door went.

I let out a sigh and pinched the bridge of my nose. This was going to be one heck of a day.

At noon, the whole town gathered by the river, where my brothers set up a huge tent with tables and benches inside. Indeed, it looked like everyone in Mossdale had contributed to the party, because I'd never seen so much food, ale, and wine in one place. Also, the number of cookies, truffles, and muffins was ridiculous. The children didn't wait for an invitation. They ran around with their hands and mouths full. I fully expected them to crash in a few hours.

I felt someone pull on my sleeve and looked down. It was Holly.

"How are you feeling?" I asked.

She stared at me like I'd just grown a second head. "Fine?" She held up a scarf. It was so large and heavy that in her arms, it looked like a blanket. "I'm going to have to ask you to cover your eyes."

"Why?" They'd never asked me to cover my eyes before. What was it that I wasn't supposed to see until the time was right?

"Please," she whined sweetly. "Pretty please? For me?" Then she touched her belly. "For the baby?"

I shook my head but took the scarf from her. "Okay. For the baby." I tied it over my eyes and soon felt Holly's small hand in mine.

She started guiding me towards the center of the tent. Everyone went silent. Only the children kept laughing and chasing each other. Their parents tried to shush them with little success.

What was that thumping in my ears? Oh. My heart. It beat uncomfortably fast, and I found myself sweating. It was a sunny day, but a bit chilly. My brothers had erected the tent in case it rained later. The year before, it had rained all day, and we'd all had to go inside. To be fair, I'd enjoyed it more than I was probably going to enjoy today. Instead of being the center of attention, like I was now, for some reason I had yet to comprehend, I got to spend the day with my close family. My brothers, my sisters-in-law, my nieces, and my nephew. They meant so much to me.

Holly stopped, and I stopped too, feeling like I was going to be sick if they didn't reveal the surprise within the next five seconds. The anticipation was too much, especially when I didn't know if whatever they'd planned was going to be good, or... not very inspired.

Not that my brothers didn't know me and didn't know what I liked and didn't like. But they often enjoyed ignoring my preferences. It was all good fun, though. I hoped today was going to be the same.

"You can take off the blindfold," Holly said.

With trembling fingers, I undid the knot. I opened my eyes, curiosity mixed with anxiety making my body buzz.

I was face to face with... a cake.

It wasn't as big as Orion, but it was an impressive cake, nonetheless. It was, maybe, twice as tall as a human, and I was certain it was going to feed the whole valley.

However... I was missing the surprise. It was just a cake.

My brothers' wives had made me cakes before. This one didn't seem to be any diff–

The top of it popped open. I gasped and involuntarily took a step back, then looked around to make sure there were no females or children I might've bumped into. It was never a good idea for a giant like me to accidentally bump into a tiny human woman.

"Surprise!" Everyone cheered at once, clapping and jumping.

And that was when the most beautiful, ethereal creature I'd ever seen jumped out of the cake. With her arms spread wide and a bright smile on her lips, she fixed me with her gaze and said, "Happy Birthday, Branthor!"

"What is this?"

No one heard me. They were all too busy wishing me a Happy Birthday and... Congratulations?

"Well, aren't you going to take your bride out of the birthday cake?" Kairos asked.

"My... what?!"

"Your bride! Congratulations, brother!" He patted me on the back, then turned away before I could bombard him with questions.

"Congratulations," Pearl and Coral, my nieces, said in unison.

I gave them an awkward smile. What was happening? What sort of crazy dream was this? I had half the mind to slap myself hard over the face to hopefully wake up.

I made my way towards the huge cake, where the blonde, delicate woman awaited. My bride.

No. Impossible. This was a prank. It had to be.

She couldn't be my bride because I... Well, because a bride was the last thing I wanted.

Teal

I had never felt more embarrassed and out of place in my life! The whole town was here, and I was stuck in a birthday cake, silently pleading with Branthor to snap out of it and help me out. Silently pleading with him to... accept me as his bride. As his gift, if he wanted to see me that way. Just accept me.

He advanced towards me, as if in a daze. His deep green eyes raked over my body. I was tiny compared to him, and he had to bend down to reach me.

"I'm sorry about this," he said.

I let out a breath of relief. Okay, so he thought it was weird, too.

"I assume you want out," he said.

"Out of the cake, yes," I said quickly. Not out of the marriage in case that was the hidden implication of his words.

He nodded and offered me his hand. I took it with both my hands, but I still didn't see how I could jump out of the thing without ruining it and breaking a leg. It was a real cake, in fact. Only the top was fake, and the compartment inside which I was standing – they were both made of cardboard. But the outside was made of thick, spongy cake, cream in three different colors, fluffy frosting, and copious amounts of fresh berries. It was a work of art, to be honest.

Everyone was looking at us.

He noticed and frowned. He didn't like this situation any more than I did.

"May I?" he asked politely.

"Huh?"

"I'll just lift you up. It's easier that way. If we ruin the cake, Holly, Nova, and Maren will kill me. Yes, on my birthday."

I laughed. "Okay."

His hands went around my waist, and he lifted me so easily that I felt like a feather. No. Actually, I felt like a toy. When he set me on the ground, I realized I barely reached his waist. He was twice as tall as any human man I'd ever met, and I honestly shouldn't have been surprised. After all, his brother, Kairos, was tall. But for some reason, when he'd told me the night before that Branthor was the youngest in their family, I'd imagined he'd be shorter. Silly me. That logic made zero sense.

Branthor was huge. Looking up at him was no easy feat. I could already feel tension in my neck and back. He had long, dark brown hair, and a long, messy beard. My fingers itched to touch it and see if it was as soft as it looked. But his most striking feature were his eyes, so green and expressive that I could lose myself in them and forget why I was here and what I was doing.

Was he handsome? Hm. Did I consider Branthor, the grendel giant handsome? In fact, he was just a grendel, not giant. Holly had explained it to me. Us humans tended to call their species giants, or forest giants, but they were grendels. Was my grendel husband handsome?

That was an easy answer. Yes. He was tall, with wide shoulders, a strong chest, well-defined abs, and arms as thick as tree trunks. I could see the veins bulging, and that sent a shiver through my body. I had no idea how this was going to work, considering the massive size difference, but I couldn't deny I was excited to find out. He was a fine specimen, Branthor.

Even finer than his brothers, who were clearly older than him.

"Are you hungry," he asked.

"Yes."

"Then we should... um... eat."

He was so awkward. Which was great because I was awkward, too. This whole situation was unusual. He gestured for me to walk ahead, and when we reached the main table, he pulled the chair for me. And I stared at it, not knowing what to do. The chairs were high. Like... so high that I had no idea how I was supposed to climb up.

"Sorry, my bad," he said as he pushed the chair back and pulled another one. "I'm not used... to this."

This chair was even higher, and it had a ladder on the side. I looked at the two chairs in astonishment, then at the humans, grendels, and their hybrid children around us. The grendels were sitting in highchairs that were wide and sturdy, while the women were sitting in these even higher chairs with ladders on the sides, which weren't as wide and as massive. The children could have their pick, depending on their age. The older children were tall, big, and heavy enough to use the sturdy chairs, and they had no trouble climbing in them without the assistance of a ladder.

"Are you okay... um..."

I blinked at him. "Teal." I realized that I knew his name, but we hadn't been properly introduced. Of course, his brothers hadn't told him my name. "My name is Teal. And yes, I think I'm okay... Or I will be." I chuckled awkwardly.

"Teal." His expression changed. He looked more... relaxed. "What a beautiful name."

"Thank you. It was my mother's choice."

"Like your eyes."

I pointed a finger at him and winked. "Good catch." Then felt like an idiot. "Um..." I looked up at the chair. Well, what was I waiting for? An official invitation?

I started climbing the ladder, and when I reached the top, I had to admit I was feeling a little... dizzy. The ladder wasn't that high, really, but I'd never been a fan of heights. I tried to make myself comfortable, but it was almost impossible. I found that my knees were trembling and feeling weak, and there was a knot in my stomach. I was hungry, but I was also scared. What if I slipped and fell?

Branthor sat down beside me and immediately started piling food onto my plate. Everyone at the table and the tables around us were chatting loudly and laughing. Noticing that they weren't staring at us anymore, I allowed myself to relax a little.

This was my home now. This was my town. Mossdale. It was beautiful, and the people living here were friendly and welcoming. I was grateful I wasn't the only human woman. On the contrary, there were a lot of us. Seeing the other women feeling so at ease, moving so freely and confidently, existing in this space like they belonged here, I felt a little better.

"We're so thrilled to finally meet you," a cute brunette with straight, shoulder-length hair said from across the table. "My name is Nova. I'm Ragnar's wife." She pointed at the grendel sitting next to her. He had a toddler in his lap. I could only tell the boy was a toddler compared to the height of the other children. "And this is Maverick. Holly and Kairos have told us so much about you! We wanted to visit you at their house last night, but they said it was better to not attract attention. This one," she pointed at Branthor, "was basically spying on us, freaking out that we were plotting something terrible."

"Nefarious," Branthor said.

Nova laughed out loud, and another woman with reddish-blonde hair joined her.

"Sorry, I'm Maren," she said, extending a hand towards me. I did the same, but our hands couldn't meet over the large table. That made her laugh harder. "Eight years living in Mossdale, and I'm still not used to the sheer size of things," she said. "I'm Orion's wife." She pointed at him. He waved at me, and I waved back. "And these are my lovely girls, Coral and Pearl." The girls were a little shy, and they barely waved and murmured a "hi". "Coral is six years old, and Pearl is four," she added helpfully, probably noticing the confusion on my face.

"It's so nice to meet everyone," I said. And I wasn't lying. It was nice, indeed, to be part of a family where there were so many women.

I looked over at Branthor, who was pouring me a glass of what looked like beer. His thick brows were furrowed, and he was silent and focused. I wanted this so badly.

I wanted him to like me, accept me, want me, take me into his home and never leave me. Because this place, this family, this community... I hadn't known something so good, and beautiful, and honest existed. I wanted to be a part of it.

Branthor noticed me watching him.

"Is this okay?" he asked. "You don't drink ale? It's a bit bitter, it's true."

I shook my head. "Ale is fine. Thank you."

"Maybe you don't like boar meat?"

I looked at my plate. "I... I don't know. It smells amazing, so I think I'll love it."

"Good," he said, turning to his plate and stabbing a fork into a huge slab of meat. "I just hope you like the food."

"And the cake, later," Holly said.

"Everything is incredible," I said. "It all looks and smells divine."

Branthor gave me a small smile, but quickly stuffed his mouth with food. Following his lead, I cut a piece of boar stake and placed it on my tongue. I was not prepared for the explosion of flavors.

As we ate, however, it wasn't lost on me that Branthor wasn't keen on making conversation. For a man who'd just been gifted a bride who'd popped out of his birthday cake, he looked... not so thrilled.

On the contrary, he seemed lost in thought. And distant.

I remembered the marriage contract that Kairos had signed in his stead.

This union was not set in stone.

Branthor

The day dragged on and on. Normally, I loved parties, but this was not a party. This was a funeral. My funeral.

After we ate, my brothers cut the cake, and everyone got a piece. I'd hoped the party would end with the cake, but no such luck. A few grendels brought in drums and string instruments, and until late at night, there was music and dancing. I was not in the mood to participate.

The little human, Teal, never left her chair. I got a feeling she didn't feel comfortable at all and didn't know what to do with herself. Holly, Nova, and Maren invited her to dance, but she refused. When they tried to convince me, I refused too.

"Come on, Branthor," Orion said, annoyed that I was refusing the females. "This is your birthday. Act like it."

"Not my birthday. You've turned it into something else," I grumbled under my nose. If Orion heard me, he didn't let on.

Teal didn't hear me, and I was grateful. Everything was too loud for her. She looked downright confused as she watched the grendels dance with their wives, and the children running around, the sugar crush not having happened yet.

"It's not usually this loud," I said to her, leaning in, so she could hear me.

Her eyes snapped up to meet mine. She was gorgeous! A gentle little thing, completely innocent and naïve in this environment. I couldn't believe she was my mate. How did my brothers steal my blood and send it to the Temple? I'd have to ask them when this monstrosity of a party was over. They had a lot of explaining to do.

Anyway, how was it possible that Teal was my perfect match? I'd heard over and over that the DNA test never got it wrong, and I had to admit that Kairos and Holly were perfect together, just like Ragnar and Nova, and Orion and Maren. My brothers had found their brides through the Marriage Temple, so it was silly of me to think the Temple had gotten me the wrong woman.

But how would it even work? A gust of wind could knock Teal down! I was afraid to breathe too hard in her direction.

"It's lovely," she said, raising her voice over the music. "I've never been to a party before."

I cocked an eyebrow. "Really?"

She nodded. "I know, it's ridiculous. We didn't celebrate things in my family."

"Not even birthdays?"

"Nope. My family was all about work, work, work. We didn't have time to do any fun stuff."

"That sounds... sad."

The corners of her mouth turned downward, and it surprised me to notice an uncomfortable feeling in my chest. Why did I care that she was sad and had never been to a party before? Sure, the Temple had found her for me, but that didn't change the fact that I didn't want a bride.

"Excuse me," I said and stood up. "I'll be back in a bit."

"Okay."

She clung to her chair even harder, her hands holding tightly onto the edges. Her cute, tiny feet in simple boots dangled in the air. It struck me that it was hard to walk away when she looked so lost and helpless. I could tell she was afraid of being so high off the ground, but too proud to say anything. Now that I was going to leave her for a few minutes, I wondered if she felt even more scared because I wasn't going to be there in case she slipped.

She wasn't going to slip. She was fine. What was wrong with me thinking that she actually needed me? We'd only known each other for a few hours, and this wasn't going to last, anyway. Why? Because I said so.

I first grabbed Kairos by the arm, then motioned for Orion and Ragnar to follow us. I led them out of the tent and towards the shore, where hopefully, no one would hear us. The sun was about to set. Fortunately, it hadn't rained today, but it could still rain during the night.

"I can't believe you did this to me," I said through gritted teeth, barely containing my displeasure.

"Did what to you?" Ragnar laughed. "Found you the most beautiful creature that your grumpy self actually doesn't deserve?"

"The most beautiful creature?" Orion said. "I thought that was your wife, Nova."

"And I thought it was your wife, Maren," Ragnar retorted.

I rolled my eyes. I didn't have the time or disposition for their shenanigans.

"That would, in fact, be my wife, Holly," Kairos said.

"Would you stop this?" I raised my voice to let them know I meant business. "I told you so many times that I do not want to get married. Did you think I was joking? Did you think it was just a phase and it would pass? Because let me tell you, no, I wasn't joking! I do not want a bride. I do not want to start a family."

My brothers were silent for a minute. At least I was getting through to them. Finally!

When it looked like no one knew what to say, Kairos shook his head, "We don't understand you, brother. You're sixty. It's time for you to settle down."

"First of all," I said, "Sixty is young. And two, you don't get to decide when I settle down, or if I settle down at all."

"You know, sometimes we wonder," said Orion, "You're not one of those grendels who're against mating with humans because the children don't grow as tall and big as us, are you?"

That took me aback. I was appalled. "What?"

"Because that's not cool," Orion continued. "Not cool at all."

"We just want our children to be happy and healthy," Ragnar said. "Even when they are a pain in the ass."

Orion shot him a look. "Only Maverick is a pain in the ass, brother. Coral and Pearl are the sweetest."

Ragnar shrugged. "I won't argue with that."

"Wait," I said. "You think that's why I don't want to get married? Are you serious? Do you think I secretly hate your children because they're hybrids?"

"We're just saying," Kairos exchanged a quick glance with Orion and Ragnar. "We don't get you, that's all. What else could it be?"

"I don't hate your children! I adore them! And I don't care if grendels shrink to the size of humans in a few hundred years! We'll build smaller houses and chop down less trees. In fact, I think that the biggest a species is, the more damage it does to the planet. Which, let's face it, isn't doing great after the Shift."

"Then what's wrong with you, Branthor?" Orion said, exasperation evident in his voice. "You can't just... live alone."

"Why not?"

"Because it's sad!"

That made me cringe. It reminded me of how Teal had told me she'd never been to a party before, and how I thought that was sad.

"I have my reasons," I said.

In unison, they crossed their arms over their huge chests.

Great! Now I had to spell it out to them. As if I hadn't been saying this for years!

"Human females are too small. Too fragile. Just look at Teal! I can't be responsible for that gentle, tiny thing! What if I hurt her?"

As if on cue, they started laughing at the same time.

"Are you serious?" Ragnar said. "You'd rather live and die alone than share your life with a beautiful woman who will bring sunshine into your home? Just because she's... small?"

I averted my gaze and scratched the back of my neck. "No? Yes? I don't know. I have no idea how it works between you and your wives."

That made them laugh even harder.

"Don't worry, brother," Kairos said. "I got you a couple of books from the Temple. You'll learn how to handle Teal in no time."

"Books?"

"Yes, they have books. They're optional, but they help."

"Oh," Orion turned to Kairos, "You didn't forget to get the oil, did you?"

"Of course not! It's among Branthor's gifts." He looked at me, annoyed. "Why haven't you opened your gifts yet? There's a mountain of them in the tent."

"What oil are you even talking about?" I asked, confused.

"You don't know?" Orion asked. "How do you think Maren and I make it work, huh? How do you think she was able to push out two perfect babies?"

"I... I..." I hadn't thought about it too much, to be fair. It didn't seem appropriate for me to be thinking about how my brothers and their wives... well... fucked.

"The oil helps things... fit," said Kairos. "You're right. Human females are tiny and frail. We must be careful. But there are books you can read to learn about their anatomy, and the Temple provides this special oil that will help matters when... the time comes, and you decide to... um... well... make Teal yours."

I covered my face with my hands and stayed like that for a minute. Finally, I let out a groan and raked my fingers through my long, tangled hair.

"No. I don't need books, and I don't need a special oil. Because she's going back. I don't want a bride. I never wanted one, and it was wrong of you to force her on me."

"She's your perfect match," Kairos said. "Brother, we did this for you."

"I am perfectly fine on my own," I said.

"No, you're not." Orion's voice turned serious. "You're lonely, Branthor. Before Kairos brought Holly, it was okay because you were both single, but now that all of us are married, we can see that something has changed in you."

I squinted my eyes at them. "Is it because I visit too often? Is that it? I won't come over to your houses anymore."

"No, that's not it. Why are you so stubborn?" Ragnar looked like he was about to lose his patience. "You can come over whenever you want. You're always welcome. We love you, Branthor, and that's why we can tell that you're not happy on your own. We know how amazing it is to be with a woman you love and who loves you back, and we want that for you."

I shook my head. "No. Forget about it. You had no right to go over my head, and I don't appreciate it. It doesn't matter you had good intentions." I turned my back on them. Before walking away, I added, "I'll take Teal to the Temple tomorrow."

I took her to my house first.

What else was I supposed to do with her? It had been a long day, and she needed a place to sleep. Plus, I hadn't told her about my decision yet. I had to do that too, and I wasn't looking forward to it. My brothers had caused this mess, and now I had to deal with it. In what world was it fair?

"Whoa! This place is huge!"

She stopped in the middle of the living room, her eyes wide. She didn't know what to look at first. To me, my house was normal. Sure, the ceiling was high, the furniture was massive, and in the middle of it all, she looked like a tiny thing. But I wouldn't have called the place... huge.

"I will prepare your room."

"My room?" her eyes snapped to mine. "I thought we'd share yours?"

I clenched my jaw and chose to not reply to that. Instead, I invited her to make herself comfortable on the couch, then disappeared into the second bedroom.

My house only had one floor, and it was small compared to my brothers' houses. It had never been my plan to start a family, so I saw no point in living in a big house. This was enough for me. Two bedrooms, two bathrooms, a kitchen with a pantry, a generous living room, a porch that stretched around the house, and a backyard where I grew my veggies and berries.

Gardening calmed me down and gave me a sense of purpose.

I kept the second bedroom clean, in case any of my brothers annoyed his wife to the point where she kicked him out. It had happened once to Ragnar when Nova was pregnant with Maverick.

I changed the sheets now, fluffed the pillows for Teal, then made the fire. It was cold outside, and the nights were going to be cold for a while, still. I heard the rain pattering gently on the windows.

"So, this is where I'll sleep?"

My heart skipped a beat. I turned to see Teal standing the doorway, watching me as I stocked the fire. I was impressed at how silently she moved. Like a cat.

"There's a bathroom down the hall," I said. "It's all yours. Feel free to take a bath."

"Thanks."

She entered the room, paced the floor for a bit, then sat down on the edge of the bed.

"Um... can you give me anything that I can wear?"

I frowned. "Where are your things? Kairos probably forgot to bring your bags. I'll go get them."

She blushed, and I found I couldn't look away from her rosy cheeks. "I have no things. I got this dress from the Temple. It's nicer than mine was."

"What? You have no things? No clothes? No shoes?"

She shook her head. "It's complicated. I had to... um... leave in a hurry. I didn't get to pack."

Why did I feel like she wasn't telling me everything? For a second, I felt the impulse to ask her. I wanted to know who she was, where she came from, and how come she didn't own a single thing. But then I reminded myself that she was only staying the night, and tomorrow I was taking her back to the Temple.

"I'll bring you something," I said. "It will probably be big for you, but comfortable to sleep in."

"Thanks."

I went into my bedroom to look for an old shirt, but then it didn't feel right to give her something old and worn, so I chose the newest shirt I had and brought it to her.

"I hope this will do," I said. "Tomorrow, you can borrow some clothes from my brothers' wives. I'm sure they will be happy to share."

She nodded and studied the shirt for a minute, turning it over and over in her delicate hands. According to my calculations, it was going to cover her from head to toe.

"Teal," I said, approaching the bed. "I need to tell you something."

She looked up at me, and there was something in her eyes that took my breath away. They were slightly wet, like she was about to cry.

"I don't want a bride." There, it was out. It was only fair for her to know. "My brothers set me up. I told them so many times, but they didn't listen, and now... here you are."

"You don't like me?"

"No!" I took a step towards her, hands raised. "No, you're lovely! It's not you. It's me. I don't see myself as a husband, so I can't... I can't do this. I'm sorry, Teal. But you understand, don't you? This marriage wasn't my choice."

"I guess that's why it's called an arranged marriage."

She was calm. Disappointed, but calm.

Now I didn't know what to do. I hated that I had to disappoint her like this.

She let out a heavy sigh, then gave me a bright smile. "Do you have any more of that wine? The ale was nice, but I loved the wine at the party. The red one."

"Sure."

"Bring me a glass? And bring a glass for yourself."

"Okay. Why not?"

I went to fetch a bottle and two glasses. When I returned to the bedroom, Teal was wearing my shirt. It looked ridiculous on her, but at the same time... sexy. How could she be so sexy when the only parts of her body that I could see were her head and the tips of her fingers poking out of the long sleeves?

She patted the spot next to her. "Sit down. Let's drink and... I don't know. Talk about nothing. If this is the only night we spend together, let's make it pleasant, right?"

"Right."

Why did this feel like a trap?

No, she was just being friendly.

It wasn't like me to be so paranoid.

Teal

What I'd feared most was happening. Branthor didn't want me. He'd never wanted a bride, and I wasn't going to change his mind.

That didn't mean I wasn't going to try.

He poured the wine and we clinked. I scooted closer to him, until my thigh touched his. He looked down at me but didn't move away. That was a good sign. However, I needed to be careful. Play my cards right. If I even had any cards, that was. I liked to think that I did.

I had no experience seducing men. None whatsoever. I was clumsy and uncertain, but I had to do my best. This was my only chance at a different life. I needed him.

Sitting so close to him as we sipped wine and watched the flames dance in the fireplace, I felt safe for the first time in my life. Because I could feel that

Branthor was gentle. His energy was like nothing I'd sensed before. Having been raised in a house where I had to pay attention to people's moods all the time, I was extra sensitive and could tell immediately how someone felt. I could almost read minds!

So, I knew what kind of soul Branthor was. Despite his massive form, his heart was sweet and kind. The fact that his family and community loved him so much also told me he was special. If there was a single chance I could convince him to let me stay, I had to take it. I couldn't let myself be defeated so easily.

"Tell me something about yourself," I said.

He frowned. "Why?"

"So we can get to know each other a little. How about this? You share something about yourself, and I share something about myself. A fair trade."

"What would be the point?" His voice dropped to almost a whisper. "You're leaving tomorrow."

"That's true. But let's not think about that now. Tonight, we're here, together, drinking wine." I had to break through the walls he'd put up. "I'll go first. One thing about me is that... I love reading adventure books. My mother used to collect them. She kept them in the attic, and whenever she had an hour or two, she'd go up there and read. I've read all her collection."

"We have a library," he said. "All the books in it have been written by grendels, though. I don't think we have any human written books."

"I would love to read some grendel fiction."

"Really?"

"Yes! Does the library have any adventure stories?"

"I'm sure it does. I can ask Maren. She works at the library."

I beamed at him. "That would be amazing."

He averted his gaze. "But you're leaving... I don't think she'll agree to lend you books you won't be able to return."

Damn it. His mind went there again. I had to find a way to distract him every time he reminded me – and himself – that he was taking me back to the Temple tomorrow.

"Oh," I said, simply. After a few seconds of silence, I changed the subject. "It's your turn. Tell me something about yourself."

"I love gardening."

"For real?"

"Yes. It calms me down, keeps me grounded. I love working with my hands, getting my hands dirty, and then seeing beautiful things grow. In my spare time – and I have a lot of it – I tend the flower beds, weed the herbs and vegetables, water the berries. When I'm not working in my garden, you'll usually find me in the orchards. We grow apples, pears, plums, peaches, and apricots."

"That is impressive!"

He smiled at me. "Do you like fruits?"

"I love them! I'm not much of a foodie, really, but give me fruits, and that's all I'll eat."

He looks me up and down, and I blush slightly. It feels like he's assessing every part of my body. Which isn't a bad thing. It's what I want. Too bad I'm wearing this oversized shirt that's covering, practically, everything.

"No. Fruits are nice," he said. "But you need food. Real, healthy, nutritious food. You're too small."

That made me laugh. "I'm not too small. It's just the way I'm built. My mother was built the same."

"I feel like you're talking about your mother in the past tense," he said.

I felt a knot in my throat. I took a moment to compose myself. A gulp of wine helped. "She died a few years ago. Right before I turned eighteen."

He leaned over me, his eyes filled with sadness. "I'm so sorry, Teal. My parents passed away, too. A long time ago."

"Oh. I'm sorry." I touched his arm. "At least we have something in common. It's sad that it has to be this."

He shook his head. "Losing loved ones is hard. I have my brothers, though, and their beautiful families. You're not alone in the world, are you?"

I let out a sigh. As far as I was concerned, I was alone. But I couldn't lie to him. No matter how horrible my father and my brothers were, they were my family.

"My father is still alive, and I have two older brothers."

"That is a relief."

His words made me cringe. Could I tell him the truth about them? Would he believe me? Or would he think I was trying to manipulate him? This was a tricky situation. I didn't want to lie to him, but at the same time, I didn't want him to think I was helpless. Even if I was.

"Should we play again?"

"Huh?" he looked at me, confused.

"The game. I'll tell you another thing about myself."

"Oh, okay. I guess there's no harm in it."

I snuggled closer to him and held up my glass for a top up. Now I was pressed to his side completely, and he still wasn't moving, which told me he didn't really want to put distance between us. His body radiated so much heat that the fire wasn't even necessary.

"I love cooking. My mother taught me how to cook, and every time I make one of her recipes, I feel close to her. Like she's in the kitchen with me, looking right over my shoulder."

To my surprise, he shifted and placed his big hand on my arm, pulling me closer to him.

"I'm sorry you lost her. It sounds like you were close."

"Yes. It's okay, though. I was lucky to know her and be her daughter."

"What's your favorite recipe to make?" he asked.

"Ugh, there are so many! Okay, let me think." I tucked my legs under me, leaning even more into Branthor. "Spaghetti and meatballs. I know, it's simple, but I associate it with my childhood."

"I'm sure it's delicious."

"I could make it for you."

He fell silent, and I wondered if I was pushing too hard. Again, it was safer to change the subject than wait and find out.

"Your turn," I said.

"I'm scared."

"Sorry?" I looked up at him, but he wasn't looking at me. He was staring into the fire.

"I'm scared that if I take a bride, I will hurt her."

My eyes widened. "Is that why you don't want a bride?"

"Humans are fragile." He placed his glass on the floor, then showed me his hand, palm up. "Look at this paw. What if I squeeze you too hard? What if I wanted to caress you, and instead hurt you?"

I placed my glass on the floor too, then climbed into his lap and took hold of his hand with both of mine.

"Do you know what I think?"

"What?"

"That you would never do that."

"I'm not saying intentionally. Accidentally."

"No. You're too gentle and too aware to do it accidentally." I lifted his hand to my cheek. "See? This is easy."

He brushed my face with the back of his index finger. I closed my eyes and smiled. When I let go of his hand, he didn't pull it away. Gingerly, he touched my hair. I felt him leaning in, and I opened my eyes and straightened my back, pulling my spine as tall as I could to meet him halfway.

"Teal, we shouldn't be doing this."

"Why not?"

"Tomorrow..."

"Don't think about tomorrow. Today, we're mated, aren't we?"

"I didn't sign the marriage contract," he said.

"It doesn't matter. It's only paperwork."

He bent his head towards me, and I craned my neck even more. Our faces were so close that I could feel his warm breath on my lips.

"I won't sign it," he said, but he didn't sound very convinced.

"Okay," I whispered as I closed the few inches between us and pressed my mouth to his.

I felt him sigh and relax. His big hand came to rest on my back, and he pulled me towards him. My hands came up to touch his beard. Finally! I'd wanted to thread my fingers through it all day. It was just as soft as I'd imagined. The kiss deepened, and the next thing I knew, the tip of his tongue was working on parting my lips. I opened up for him, and we tasted each other.

It was all so intense that I could feel my core melting. I hadn't been kissed or touched like this before. The few kisses I'd shared with my first and only boyfriend had been clumsy and hadn't stirred much inside me. What I was doing now with Branthor had me turned into a pathetic little puddle.

He was the one who pulled away. We stared into each other's eyes for a minute, and I thought he was going to kiss me again. The way he was looking at me... It was as if a war was waging inside him. A part of him wanted to throw all caution to the wind and take me then and there, and another part of him kept reminding him that he didn't want a bride because he was afraid. Afraid he would hurt me.

That was never going to happen, and I knew it. I'd been hurt all my life by men, and it was easy for me to tell that Branthor just wasn't that type.

His self-control was astonishing. With the utmost care, he removed me from his lap and tucked me in bed.

"Good night, Teal."

Teal

I woke up early, slipped out of Branthor's enormous shirt, and took a bath. I'd barely been able to sleep, my mind going in circles, making up possible scenarios that would convince him to give this relationship a chance. Today, I had to give it my all. I had to use all the tools I had in my arsenal, and my strongest one was... well... my body.

What I was going to do...

It was completely out of character for me. I'd never done anything like it before, but I had to try. The kiss we'd shared the night before told me the DNA test had been correct. We were made for each other. It didn't matter that I was tiny, and he was a giant. If his brothers and their wives had made it work, then we would, too. I had to make Branthor see that. See what was possible.

I got out of the tub and dried my body and my hair, then walked back into the bedroom completely naked. The clock on the wall said it was eight. I wondered if Branthor was awake already. Any minute now, he was going to knock on my door and tell me it was time to go.

The thought that later today I might find myself back at the Temple, where the priest and the Temple servants would allow me to spend one night before I had to take the train back home... It made me feel vulnerable and slightly sick to my stomach. I had to actively force myself to not think about it.

If Branthor took me back and the arranged marriage was off, that meant the Temple would return his money, too. It only made sense. His brothers' money, but that was beside the point. I would be left with nothing once more. Why had I thought that asking the priest to transfer the money to me would make any difference?

Panic was starting to set in. I couldn't drown in it, not yet. This was not the time to give up. I was still here, in Branthor's house, and there were still some things I could do to ingratiate myself with him. Last night, he'd kissed me so deeply and passionately that for a moment, I'd thought he would never let me go. The feel of his body against mine... The way I fit perfectly in his lap... Surely, he'd felt it too.

A knock on the door startled me. My instinct was to reach out for the oversized shirt and put it on, but I fought it. Branthor didn't wait for me to invite him in. He cracked the door open, and at the sight of my nakedness, instantly closed it shut. I heard him clear his throat.

"Sorry, I shouldn't have barged in like that," he said. "I just wanted to let you know breakfast is ready."

He'd made breakfast for me? My lips stretched into a grin. I pulled my shoulders back, exposing my round breasts and hardened nipples, walked to the door, took one deep breath, and opened it.

Branthor was standing in the hallway, and at the sight of me, his eyes widened. He couldn't look away. His gaze raked over my body, taking in every inch of my skin. My long neck, my small, firm breasts, my pink nipples, the triangle of my pussy that was covered in soft, blonde hair. His lips parted open, but no sound came out.

"You cooked breakfast for me?" I asked.

"Um... Leftovers from the party... I threw them together... It was no bother at all."

"Aww... That's so cute of you. I'm starving."

"Yes, I... I thought you might be hungry. Um... I'll wait for you downstairs."

He made to leave, but I stepped out of the room and stopped him. I clung to his arm.

"No 'good morning' kiss?" I purred, lifting myself on my tiptoes. Not that it helped much. I still could barely reach his navel.

"Teal." His voice was low and husky. His green eyes grew a shade darker, and for a second, I thought he was going to give in. "We can't."

"Why not?"

"Because today–"

"Today, we're still together. I am here, aren't I? And you are here, with me, and we're going to have breakfast together in a few minutes. Today, we're still mated."

"Teal, please. You're making this very hard."

"What exactly is hard, Branthor?" That was when I had the inspiration to reach below his waist and touch his cock in his rather tight cotton pants. "Oh. I get it now."

"Teal!" He took a step back. "Don't do that."

"Why not? Don't tell me you're not hard for me, because I won't believe you."

"We talked about this. I can't take a bride. I don't want a bride."

"But you want me."

He pursed his lips. No matter how insistently he was fighting the attraction between us, he couldn't look away from me. Every time he tried to avert his gaze, his eyes would snap back to me, and more often than not, he couldn't peel them off my pebbled nipples.

"Teal, don't do this to me," he said.

"What am I doing to you, Branthor?" I rubbed his cock. The length of it was impressive. "You want me. Tell me I'm wrong."

"You're not wrong."

I could feel him giving in, little by little. I could feel him growing even harder under my warm palm. And that was when I decided to pull away. I went back into the bedroom and threw over my shoulder, "I'll be down in a minute."

He blinked at me, confused. He took one step to follow me, and for a second, I thought he was going to suggest we skipped breakfast and spent the morning in bed, but then he snapped out of his lust induced daze, swallowed heavily to calm himself down, and stopped in the doorway.

"It's a lovely day," he said, "And I thought it would be nice to eat on the back porch."

"That sounds great! I can't wait for you to show me your garden."

Before he closed the door to let me get dressed, I saw a grin pull at the corners of his lips. Oh, yes, he wanted to show me his garden alright. I'd said the right thing.

I heard him walk away, and I quickly put on his oversized shirt. It dropped down to my toes, and I definitely looked better in the dress I'd worn the day before, but I figured that wearing his shirt would have a better impact.

This was going better than I'd expected. This was going great!

BRANTHOR

It was hard to take my eyes off her. She was wearing the shirt I'd given her the night before, and it was interesting to me how this simple gesture made me feel. She could've worn the dress she had, but she'd chosen my shirt, even if she'd slept in it. She was wearing something that was mine, and I felt... proud?

Teal ravenously dug into the breakfast I'd prepared for us, and I watched her fascinated, wondering how she could be so small and eat so much. There was leftover cake from my birthday party, and she dug into that too. Meanwhile, she asked me questions about Mossdale.

"Grendels built this town after the Shift," I explained to her. "Mossdale is very old, indeed. It used to be bigger, but as time passed, the community got divided by opposing beliefs, and some chose to leave."

"What opposing beliefs?"

"Some grendels wanted to take human brides and build families of their own. Others refused to even consider it as an option. The offspring of humans and grendels are hybrids that are smaller and weaker than pure blood grendels, and those who left Mossdale did so because they didn't want to dilute the blood of our ancestors. Or so they said."

"Wow! Do you know why there are so few female grendels?"

I shook my head. "No. There are theories that say something happened after the Shift that affected our genes, and less and less females were born. It's a mystery, and I'm afraid it will remain a mystery."

"And do you subscribe to the idea that your ancestors' blood should not be diluted?"

"No, not at all. I subscribe to the idea that everyone should do as they please, as long as they don't hurt anyone else."

She smiled at me. I noticed she had a smudge of cake on her left cheek, and before thinking, I reached out and wiped it with my thumb.

"Sorry, you had something there."

She chuckled. "Thank you."

I gave her a half smile. "You're welcome."

So polite. The both of us. We were here, having a lovely breakfast together, acting all nice and friendly, as if she hadn't climbed into my lap the night before and we hadn't kissed. As if she hadn't strutted around completely naked this morning and hadn't rubbed my erection through my pants.

Who was this woman? How could she be so innocent, yet so daring and enticing at the same time? She gave me whiplash, for sure.

"What is your favorite place in Mossdale?" she asked.

"There are so many places," I said. "It's hard to choose one."

"Try."

"Hm. I guess… If I really had to choose… It's an odd one, though."

"Now I'm intrigued."

"Okay. The Thundering Caves."

"The Thundering Caves? That sounds ominous."

"They're mysterious, for sure. They are carved deeply in the mountain, and no one has managed to explore every cavern and crevice. We're all convinced they hide secrets from before the Shift. Sometimes, when there is no work to be done in the garden or the orchards, I take my equipment and go down into the caves."

"That is fascinating." Her beautiful blue-green eyes were wide. She was looking at me as if she was mesmerized, and I found that I loved it. I loved all this attention she was giving me. "You must take me there sometime."

"What? No. Out of the question."

She pouted cutely, and now I just wanted to kiss her lips. "Why not?"

"It's dangerous. One time, I got lost and it took me hours to find my way back. If it's dangerous to me, it's certainly deadly to you."

"But you would be there to take care of me. I promise not to wander on my own."

I opened my mouth to protest again, then closed it. Because... what were we doing here?

"Teal, if you've finished eating..."

"Oh." She looked at the food that was left on the table, and I could tell she wasn't hungry anymore. Still, she reached for an apple. "Juicy," she said, grinning up at me.

I groaned. She was delaying the inevitable. I knew she wanted to stay and be my bride, but I had no idea why. It couldn't have been just the fact that the DNA test said we were right for each other. She was so young, so beautiful and full of life! Why would she even want to be married so soon? And to an ugly, clumsy giant like me... A woman like her needed someone pretty and fair, with a clean-shaven jaw and smooth hands. I was covered in too much hair, and my hands were calloused from doing the work I loved.

"All right, you can finish your apple," I said. To drive my point home, I stood up and started clearing the table. She pouted again, but I chose to ignore her.

As I was carrying a stack of plates into the kitchen, I heard the front door open, then the all-too-familiar sounds of Ragnar's family filled the house. He was here with Nova and Maverick. They burst into my kitchen before I could unload the dishes into the sink and go welcome them – or shoo them back home, since the last thing I needed this morning was visitors.

"Good morning, brother," Ragnar said, patting me on the back. "How was your first night as a married man?"

I rolled my eyes at him. "Nothing happened. Because I'm not married."

"Let me ask Teal, see what she says," Nova shot at me as she made her way to the back porch. Maverick followed her on his chubby, wobbly legs.

I made to go after them, but Ragnar stopped me. He pulled me into the living room, and I didn't appreciate it. I wanted to know what Nova and Teal were talking about. Me, of course. They were going to talk about me, and Teal was going to tell her how we'd kissed.

No. Why would she do that? That was an intimate thing that had happened between us and only concerned us.

Why was I so worried about the two females gossiping about me?

Teal would never. She wasn't that kind of person.

"I brought you some reading material," Ragnar said, presenting me with two books. "I recommend you read this one first."

"What is this?" The title was self-explanatory, but I was more interested in why my brother thought I needed it.

"It's a very practical, very succinct guide on human anatomy. You'll learn everything you need to know in no time. Now, this other book..." He tapped the cover and gave me a wink. "This one you're going to like. Read it carefully."

It was called "The Art of Pleasing Your Bride", and I could only imagine what it contained.

I took the books from him and dumped them on the living room table.

"Don't forget to take them back when your little, unwelcome visit is over," I said.

Ragnar sighed. I felt exasperation coming off him in waves, but I wasn't going to back down. He was overstepping here, and this was my house. And my life.

"Why are you being so stubborn, Branthor? It's not funny anymore, you know."

"It was never intended to be funny."

"Do you really not like Teal? Do you not want her here?"

I hesitated. How was I supposed to answer that? With the truth?

What was the truth?

She was delightful. The most incredible creature I'd ever met. When we were together, I forgot that I'd never wanted a bride. Suddenly, it made sense to have her in my life. And it hadn't even been twenty-four hours!

When he saw that I had no words, Ragnar smiled rather deviously.

"Kairos will drop by a bit later to bring you the oil. You will need it."

Right. I hadn't unpacked my birthday gifts yet.

I heard the females in the kitchen. Eager to know what they were doing, I turned my back on my brother and followed Teal's cheerful laughter. If I could hear that sound for the rest of my life, I'd be a happy man.

No. I couldn't think like that. I'd made a decision, and I wasn't going to back down.

"I have a few clothes from before I got pregnant with Maverick that will fit you," Nova was saying. "When I came to Mossdale, I was tiny like you. Not anymore."

"What are you talking about?" Teal said. "You look amazing."

Nova laughed. "Who said I didn't look amazing?"

"Sorry." Teal blushed.

"What's happening?" I asked.

"Oh, I'm stealing Teal so she can choose some stuff from my wardrobe," Nova said. "You don't mind, do you? I promise to bring her back by lunch."

I frowned. "By lunch?"

"Why?" Nova challenged. "You have somewhere to be?"

I crossed my arms over my chest. Teal was looking at me with hope in her eyes. She was bouncing on her feet, excited to go with Nova and check out her clothes. How could I shatter her joy? I couldn't.

"Fine," I said. "You can take Teal."

"Great!" Nova took Teal's hand, then looked up at her husband. "Watch Maverick, will you? Us girls need a little quality time on our own."

I could tell that Ragnar wasn't happy. I rolled my eyes and took Maverick in my arms.

"Don't worry, Nova, I got this one. He'll help me in the garden."

"Thank you, Branthor. You're going to be the best dad in the world."

She pulled Teal out of the kitchen before I could say anything.

"While you and Maverick get your hands dirty, let me read you the first chapter in 'The Art of Pleasing Your Bride'," Ragnar said.

"No."

"I will read, and you will listen."

I let out a groan as I carried Maverick outside. It was impossible to get these people off my back!

And now I had to postpone taking Teal to the Temple. I was pretty sure Nova wasn't going to bring her back before lunch, like she'd said, and Teal would have to spend the whole day and another night in Mossdale.

Teal

Nova hadn't been completely honest. Yes, she'd brought me to her house to show me her clothes and let me choose what I wanted to borrow, but she'd also brought me for a girls' meeting with Holly and Maren. They were waiting in the kitchen, brewing tea, and chattering away. When they saw me, they welcomed me with open arms and kissed me on both cheeks, as if we were family already.

"Tell us everything about last night," Holly said, awkwardly climbing in one of the chairs. Seeing how big her baby bump was, I doubted it was a good idea for her to keep doing this.

"There's nothing to tell," I said. I climbed in another chair just as awkwardly, while Nova and Maren had no issue whatsoever. "Branthor made the bed and the fire in the second bedroom, and we slept separately. He doesn't want to sign the marriage contract. Had Nova not intervened and literally kidnapped me from his house, I would be on my way to the Temple."

"Nonsense," Maren said. "He won't send you back."

"That's what he said," I shrugged. "He sounds convinced. I believe him."

"Do you want to stay?" asked Holly.

"Yes."

"Then he has no say in it," she smiled sweetly.

"Men," Nova said, "They think they make the decisions, when they have no idea."

The girls laughed, and I laughed with them, though I was pretty sure they didn't know how stubborn Branthor could be. It seemed to me like they were dismissive of his stubbornness, which made them a tiny bit blind to reality.

"I don't know," I said. "I tried my best to show him we can be good together, but it only worked up to a point."

Holly wiggled her eyebrows at me. "What did you do?"

I blushed. "Sorry, can't give you details."

"Girl, did you kiss?" Maren asked.

"Yes..."

"Then it's settled. You are mates, and whatever he says doesn't matter." Maren sipped her tea, proud of herself, as if she'd just fixed my problem.

These women really liked to meddle. I found that cute. And I didn't mind it if their meddling made Branthor see that our marriage was meant to happen, but right now, I just didn't see things going in that direction.

"He'll come around," Nova said in a gentle tone.

I nodded and sipped my own tea. It was rather bitter, so I added a teaspoon of honey.

"If you have any advice on how to make him like me," I said.

"Like you? Girl, he is mad about you," Maren said.

I wasn't sure whether what Maren displayed was positivity or delusion. It did make me feel better, though. Like what I wished could be possible. Maybe soon, I would be part of their family.

"Anyway, I'm open to suggestions," I said.

"Okay, do you know what grendels like most?" Holly said. "To be climbed like trees."

"What?" I nearly choked on my tea.

"Oh, they love that," Nova agreed. "It makes them feel strong."

"Why would I... climb Branthor like a tree?" I asked.

Holly shrugged. "I once climbed Kairos because I saw a spider on the ceiling and wanted to save it and put it outside. He's clumsy with his big hands, so I had to catch the spider in a jar."

I laughed out loud. "That's ridiculous."

"Ridiculous, but it worked," Holly grinned at me. "Once the spider was safely outside, Kairos threw me over his shoulder and rushed me into the bedroom."

Warmth spread through my body when I imagined Branthor throwing me over his shoulder.

"I insist on being the one to hang the curtains after we wash them," said Nova, "so Ragnar lets me climb him to do it. I tell him it's because he hangs them all wrong, but that's not true." She winked at me.

"Okay, so I have to come up with a pretext."

"Make it a good one," said Holly. "Guaranteed success."

My mind was already coming up with scenarios. I could use Holly's trick and pretend I saw a spider on the ceiling. Would Branthor play along? I had to admit the idea of climbing him like a tree in hopes it would turn him on was... out of the box. My fear of heights was going to have to suck it up. My happiness was on the line, here.

"How about we choose some nice clothes for you?" Nova said.

The girls climbed out of their chairs. I climbed down too, slower and clumsier, and followed them into the bedroom. Nova and Ragnar's house was bigger than Branthor's. It was obvious they'd built it with a big family in mind. I doubted they were going to stop at Maverick.

The main bedroom was massive and bright. There was a four-poster bed that was bigger than anything I'd ever seen, and when Nova went to open the doors to the closet, I realized it was a walk-in closet. I gasped, then covered my mouth with my hand when I saw the other women were behaving like this was totally normal. They probably had humongous walk-in closets, too. As for me, I'd only had an old trunk at the foot of my bed where I stored my clothes, which, apparently, had never even been mine.

I followed Nova, Holly, and Maren inside. There were rows upon rows of clothes displayed on hangers. On the right side, Ragnar's clothes, and on the left side, Nova's. She started pulling out dresses, pants, and shirts, and Holly and Maren held them up for me to see.

"These should be your size," Nova said. "I won't fit in them again, so you can have them."

"Oh, no. I'll give them back."

She laughed. "No way, I won't accept them. Keep them, wear them, love them, take care of them. I'm glad I don't have to throw them out."

Holly looked at herself in the mirror that occupied the entirety of the back wall.

"Yeah," she said. "I should give you some of my clothes, too. After the baby is born, I don't think I'll fit into them either."

"Don't say that," I said. "You'll get your body back."

Maren shook her head. "Not really. A pregnancy with a baby that's half-grendel changes you. Like, it changes everything in your body. Chemistry, hormones, even your anatomy. Not by a lot, but you will notice you're not the same. After Coral and Pearl, I could swear I was bigger and even... taller. It makes no sense, but it's true."

"So true," said Nova. "I felt the same after Maverick. I also think it's because of the oil."

"The oil?"

"Oh, this dress will look lovely on you," Nova squealed, suddenly losing interest in what we were talking about. "Try it on."

"Now?"

"Yes!"

It was a short, white dress with a floral print. The girls took the clothes they'd chosen for me and walked out of the closet to give me space and some privacy. Having no other choice, I slipped out of Branthor's oversized shirt and put on the dress. It barely covered my butt. When I went into the bedroom to show them, they squealed and clapped excitedly.

"Climb Branthor in that, and you'll have him wrapped around your little finger."

"Let me get you some shoes," Nova said.

She gave me a pair of simple, black ballet flats, and my outfit was complete. It was a good thing it was sunny and warm outside.

"Let's add a scarf," Holly said, as if she could read my mind. "Just in case it gets chilly later."

The girls folded the clothes for me, and I didn't know how to thank Nova. No one had given me so much stuff before and asked for nothing in return. As we walked out of the bedroom, the front door opened. Ragnar and Maverick were home. Branthor followed them inside, his eyes scanning the living room for me.

When his eyes fell on me in the short, flimsy dress, I could swear he stopped breathing. I gave him the sweetest smile I could muster and spun in place for him. The skirt lifted an inch higher and showed more of my long, pale legs.

"What do you think?" I asked. "Do you like it? Nova said I can keep it."

He was speechless.

"Are you guys hungry?" Nova asked. "I can prepare a snack."

"Not hungry," Branthor said in a strained voice. "We just had breakfast."

I thought for a second. The right answer was that I wasn't hungry, either. The idea was to be alone with Branthor, so I could charm him, not use his family as buffer.

"I'm stuffed," I told Nova. "I ate too much for breakfast. Thank you for the tea and the clothes."

"You're welcome, Teal."

"Come," Branthor said. "It's time to go."

My heart sank. I waved at the girls, then followed him outside. It seemed like he was out of patience. The dress and the girls' advice to try and climb him like a tree weren't going to work.

"Will you take me back to the Temple now?" I asked him as we made our way to his house.

Branthor didn't say anything and didn't look at me. He looked straight ahead, and he seemed to be… lost in thought.

Branthor

"I've changed my mind," I said. I opened the door for her, and she walked into the house. "You can leave the clothes here, and we can go for a walk, if you want."

"Wait. What do you mean... you changed your mind?"

She was looking at me with those beautiful blue-green eyes that made me weak in the knees.

"You can stay another day. And night."

"Oh."

"I won't sign the marriage contract," I hurried to make it clear to her. "But I can see how much fun you're having, and I don't want to cut it short for you. You seem to love Mossdale..."

"I do love it."

"So, do you want me to show you around?"

"Yes, please. I'd love that."

She didn't sound as excited as I'd hoped she'd be. I thought my decision to let her stay another day would fill her with joy, but the truth was… it didn't fill me with joy, either. In the pit of my stomach, I had this sense of dread. She had to leave, though. She couldn't stay. I reminded myself over and over that I did not want a bride.

My brothers were great husbands and fathers, but I saw how much work that was. Was I ready to give up my freedom and dedicate myself to building a family? No. I was too used to being on my own. I was fine on my own, too. Just great.

One more day, and my life would be back to normal.

We strolled down the main road towards the river. It was a beautiful day, and Teal looked ethereal in her flowery dress. She walked ahead, curiously admiring the houses and the gardens, saying "hi" to grendels, their wives and their children when we passed them by. I couldn't take my eyes off her delicate form. Her pale legs were thin and long, and the bright sun made her skin shine so bright that it almost looked ivory. Her white-blonde hair bounced over her shoulders, and she regularly tucked it behind her ear – a gesture

I found fascinating. It was nice to walk a few steps behind her and observe her. The best part was that she had no idea I was watching her. Every time she turned around to tell me something, I quickly averted my gaze.

"Good day to you, Branthor and Teal! What a beautiful couple you make."

Damn in. Sava and Varna, the only female grendels in Mossdale were waving at us from their porch. Teal turned to them and waved, and they invited us over.

"Come have a cup of tea with us."

Teal looked at me with hope in her eyes. She'd just interacted with male grendels, and she was curious about the females. I couldn't say no to her. I nodded, and she clapped her hands and skipped to Sava and Varna.

"Hi! Thank you for inviting us."

"It's lovely to have you in Mossdale, Teal," Sava said. "This old grump needed some sunshine in his life."

I rolled my eyes. Sava and Varna were sisters. They'd come to Mossdale from one of the other grendel communities, leaving their sons behind. Why? Because their sons were against taking human brides, and Sava and Varna had wanted grandkids. Since they weren't going to have them, they chose to move to Mossdale, where they knew they would be surrounded by hybrid children. The two females were lovely, and we all adored them. However, they could be nosey. They rarely minded their own business.

"Tell us," Varna said, leaning in towards Teal, who was struggling to find her balance on the highchair. "How do you like Branthor so far?"

I let out a groan that I masked by taking a sip of tea. But I couldn't deny I was curious to hear Teal's answer.

"Um... I like him," she said. "He's sweet, and thoughtful, though he's trying really hard to hide it."

"That's our Branthor," Sava said.

"You're walking awfully well, though," Varna said with a disapproving glance at Teal's hips and legs. "No wobbling, no wincing... You got into that chair with no trouble at all."

"What do you mean?"

I blanched. I knew exactly what Varna was going to say next. I looked around us, trying to come up with a way out. Would it be too dramatic if I hauled Teal onto my shoulder and ran out of here?

"Holly's first day here…" Sava chuckled. "She could barely walk!"

"Oh. Why?"

"Kairos brought her from the Temple, took her straight to his bed, and poor thing, in the morning she was wobbling around, wincing at every step, trying to hide how sore she was."

The two females laughed thunderously. I, on the other hand, was seething.

Teal turned an even lighter shade of pale, if that was possible. She shot me a glance, and I mouthed "sorry." It wasn't my fault these old women could not control themselves. Sitting down for tea had been a bad idea. I should've told them we were busy, but I couldn't refuse Teal when she gave me that innocent, hopeful stare of hers.

"I… We…" Teal was at a loss for words. "We didn't… yet."

That rendered the two females silent. They fixed me with a disapproving gaze, and I knew I had to get out of there before they inflicted one of their well-intended lectures on me.

"We have to go," I said, wrapping my hands around Teal's tiny waist and lifting her off the chair.

She squealed and held on to me for dear life. "Where are we going?"

"You wanted to see the orchards, remember?"

"Oh..."

"Are you running away, Branthor?" Sava asked.

"What? Of course not."

"You're running away from two old women," Varna said, shaking her head. "When will you come around, youngling?"

That made Teal burst out in laughter.

"Thank you for the tea," I said. I mumbled a few more things but made sure they couldn't hear me. I urged Teal to walk ahead of me. Fast. "Don't mind them," I told her. "They get bored in their old age."

"I think they're funny."

"They're funny, alright."

"So, you're going to show me the orchards?"

"Yes. If you want to see them, that is. If not, we can go back to the house."

"No! Of course I want to see them. They're your happy place."

"My happy place?"

She started rambling about what a "happy place" was, but I could hardly pay attention. All I could think about was how I was digging myself deeper into this situation. This arranged marriage situation.

Earlier, when we'd returned from Nova's and Ragnar's place, she'd asked me if I was going to take her back to the Temple, and I'd said no. Not yet. How stupid could I be? Right then and there, I'd had the chance to end this, and instead I'd thought... one more day.

What damage could another day spent with Teal do?

A lot, as it turned out. Because after we strolled through the apple orchard for half an hour, she said she was tired, and I pulled her down onto the grass, in the shade of the apple trees in bloom. She rested her beautiful head on my arm and promptly fell asleep.

And now, here I was, staring at her immaculate face, feeling my heart beat to a different rhythm than before. A rhythm that I didn't know. It was all new to me. These feelings that she stirred inside me...

What else could I do than let her sleep and doze off myself? I couldn't remember ever feeling such all-encompassing peace.

TEAL

When I'd said I wanted to cook for him, I hadn't taken into account the fact that absolutely everything in Branthor's kitchen was oversized. It was a good thing the ingredients weren't. It was hard to chop an onion as it was; I didn't want to think how I might've gone about chopping a grendel-sized onion.

Branthor gave me the smallest knife he had, and I could barely wield it. As for the pots and pans, he had to maneuver them for me. So, cooking dinner for him turned into cooking dinner together. It was impossible to do without assistance.

"How do Holly, Nova, and Maren manage?" I asked.

"Oh, they have special pots and utensils made for them."

I glared at him. "And why don't you have any?"

"Because I don't–"

"Want a human bride," we said at the same time.

He frowned. I sighed. It was what it was. Right now, it was better to focus on the food than let myself spiral. At least he had ladders and chairs with ladders. It made sense, since he had three sisters-in-law who were human. When they came to visit, they had to sit somewhere.

He was a decent assistant, though. Except for when he wanted to lick the spoon clean after I used it to stir the tomato sauce.

"No." I pointed at him. "We do not lick spoons."

"Why not?" He shot me a confused glance.

"Because I say so."

"Well, do you have a good reason for this rule?"

I thought for a second. No, not really. It was just something I'd learned from my mother. When one cooked, it was natural to lick the spoon from time to time, not just to taste the food, but also to... well, clean the spoon. My mother had never done it. When I was little and had the instinct to do it, she stopped me immediately.

"It goes in the sink," I said.

"If it goes in the sink, anyway, then why can't I lick it first?"

I let out a sigh. Maybe Branthor was right. Maybe this rule made no sense, and as usual, my mother had come up with it because of how particular my father was.

"Okay, fine. You can lick it."

"Thank you," he said rather passive-aggressively, and proceeded to give the spoon a good clean with his tongue.

I watched, mesmerized. Was he putting on a show for me? What was this? And why was my core suddenly feeling warm? I squeezed my thighs together when I realized the sight of him licking the spoon turned me on. I wanted to know what it would be like to have that tongue run all over my body.

When he was done with the spoon, he dropped it in the sink.

"Delicious," he said. "Can we eat now?"

"I... I just have to mix the spaghetti in..." I was stuttering. Why was I stuttering? This was ridiculous!

"I'll help," he said.

"No. How about you set the table?"

"On the back porch?" he asked.

"Sure."

"It's a little chilly."

I gave him a mischievous smile. "I'm sure you'll find a way to keep me warm."

I'd made him my favorite – spaghetti with marinated meatballs. Did I think cooking for him was going to convince him to let me stay? It sure couldn't hurt. He helped me carry the plates to the back porch, and we sat down to have a lovely dinner. When he flicked a switch on the wall, the whole garden lit up with beautiful lights. It took my breath away.

"This is amazing."

"Do you like it?"

"I love it! It's so... romantic."

He looked at me, not knowing what to say. I chuckled and dug into my food, closing my eyes and moaning at the rich taste.

"Mm... I hope you like it," I said. "If you don't, don't feel bad about it. I will eat your portion, no problem."

"This is great," he said with his mouth full. "I mean it. Thank you for cooking, Teal."

"It was my pleasure. I love cooking, so... I have a few more recipes I think you'd love."

He was silent at that. He fell silent often, when I said something that implied I might stick around longer. We'd spent the most amazing day together, and I truly didn't understand why he was still reluctant to this arranged marriage. We were clearly good together.

Of course we were! A DNA test had matched us.

I decided to give him a break for a bit, and we chatted about other things. Insignificant things compared to the topics that really mattered. But I noticed how he slowly relaxed. After all, I wanted this evening to be special. If nothing came out of it, at least I'd have some good memories to keep me going back in the real world.

We finished eating and drank a glass of wine. I was tired and ready to go to bed, but I didn't want to move. I knew that if I went to bed, I was going to wake up in the morning, and Branthor would take me to the Temple. I didn't think he would change his mind again. I was surprised I'd gotten to spend the day with him, frankly. Considering how insistently he said he didn't want a bride, I hadn't expected him to stay glued to my side the whole day. We'd even taken a nap in the orchard.

"I'll clear the table," he said. "You go rest. I can see you're exhausted."

"Me? Exhausted? Naaaah..." My protest turned into a mighty yawn.

He smiled. "Go to bed, Teal. It was a long day."

"Not long enough," I said.

He started clearing the table, and I didn't have a choice. I went to the bathroom first and washed up, then in my bedroom, I looked at the clothes I'd left on the bed. Nova had given me many dresses and shirts, but not a single pair of pajamas. I'd have to sleep in Branthor's oversized shirt again, which didn't bother me at all. I slipped out of the dress I was wearing.

Then an idea popped right into my tired brain. What if I completely disregarded what Branthor kept saying he wanted, and went with my gut? My gut told me he desired me just as much as I desired him. So, instead of putting on his shirt and climbing into bed, I snuck into his bedroom. Naked. What was the worst that could happen?

He was going to wrap me up in the bed sheets and take me back to my room? Fine. Whatever.

I tiptoed to the massive bed that dominated the bedroom, climbed in, and snuggled in his sheets. They smelled like him. The fire was crackling in the fireplace, lulling me to sleep, but I did my best to stay awake. Soon enough, I heard him go into the bathroom, then come out. He first went into my bedroom, and when he didn't find me there, he looked for me in the living room and the kitchen, even if he'd just come from there.

"Teal? Where are you? You're not hiding, are you? What is this game?"

I couldn't help giggling. He was being so silly. Why would I hide from him? I wasn't playing any games. I wanted him, and I'd made it clear. He was the one playing games here. With me and with himself.

"In here," I called.

He came quickly, mumbling something under his breath. He was cute when he was so grumpy.

"What are you doing in my bed?" he asked.

I shrugged. "I wanted to see if it's more comfortable than mine."

"Both beds are the same."

"I don't know..." I sat up, pulling the thick, soft blankets off my shoulders. I ran a hand over his pillow. "It definitely looks and feels more comfortable."

Branthor blushed. So hard that even the tips of his ears were red.

"Are you naked under there?"

"What if I am?"

"Teal," he groaned.

But he didn't look away from me. He couldn't. He'd done the same thing this morning. His silly mouth said one thing, but his body said another. I could see his cock growing hard in his pants.

"You have so many interesting things in your room," I said. "Like... this thing on your nightstand." I took the amber-colored bottle in both my hands and studied it carefully. "What's in here?"

"Oil," he said.

My eyebrows shot up. "Oil? What kind of oil? I keep hearing people mentioning this oil, but I have no idea what it does. It's not for cooking, is it? Or it would be in the kitchen."

He laughed and finally approached the bed. He took the bottle from me and held it in his hands.

"It's for..." He was trying to find his words. He cleared his throat and tried again. "It's from the Temple. When a bride and groom must... um... manage with a size difference like ours, this oil is necessary. It's to... help the bride relax. More than that. It's to help her... well..." His gaze dropped to my pelvis.

"Oh," I said, squeezing my legs tightly. "Oh, I understand now."

"Yes."

He placed the bottle back on the nightstand. He was close enough that I could touch his arm. I stretched towards him, pushing the covers off me.

"I want to know how it feels," I said.

"Teal..."

"Please."

The look he gave me told me he couldn't say "no" to me. Not now, not ever.

BRANTHOR

"We can't do this," I said. "We shouldn't."

"Why not?"

I could feel my resolve fading. Her blue-green eyes shimmered with lust, and her pink lips were wet and trembling. Her body was naked before me, her luscious, soft skin beckoning me to touch her. Her breasts were small and round, her nipples dark pink and hard. It was impossible to resist her. Yet, I had to try.

"Teal, I'm taking you to the Temple tomorrow."

"Why, Branthor?" She clung to my arm, pulling me towards her. "Tell me why. I agree what your brothers did was not great. Going behind your back, stealing your blood to send to the Temple... But the outcome is not so bad, is it? How lucky are we to have found our match? Do you know how long I've been waiting?"

I sat next to her, and she curled her lithe body close to mine.

"No," I said.

"Five years, Branthor! I sent my blood to the Temple five years ago, and now it's finally happened. They found me a husband. And that husband is you."

Her confession took me aback. This meant she was barely eighteen when she made the choice to give herself to a monster. Why would she? Why would any eighteen-year-old prefer an arranged marriage to a normal, natural relationship with one of her kind?

"I don't understand," I said.

"It doesn't matter. I've waited for you, Branthor. Give me a good reason why I should give up on this."

"I... I..."

Suddenly, I felt silly for being so stubborn. At least she agreed what my brothers had done was not cool. It felt nice to be on the same page.

"Okay, so take me back to the Temple tomorrow," she said. "Fine. But let's spend this night together."

"Teal, we can't. You're a virgin. If you lose your virginity now, you won't be able to find another mate through the Temple."

She chuckled bitterly. "The DNA test won't find me another match, Branthor. That's not how it works. It's you. No one else."

I averted my gaze, not feeling like I could look her in the eye anymore. She was right, of course.

"Listen, I don't care," she said. "I just want tonight to be special. I want to lose my virginity to you, my perfect mate. Whatever happens after, I don't want to think about it. There will be plenty of time for that."

She took the oil from the nightstand and pushed it into my hand. She put both her hands over mine, and her warmth seeped into my skin. If her hands on mine could make my blood boil like this, how would it feel to have her entire naked body pressed to mine? How would it feel to be inside her?

I bent over and kissed her hands. She sighed and reached up to touch my face. I closed my eyes and let her explore my cheeks, my forehead, the bridge of my nose. Her fingers were like butterfly wings – so gentle and delicate.

"Look at me," she said.

I shook my head, refusing to open my eyes.

"Look at me, Branthor."

I didn't want to. Because she was so sweet and perfect, and I was being selfish. I wanted her, but at the same time, I couldn't make peace with the fact that if I let this arranged marriage happen, my life would never be the same. I'd been so convinced I would never get married. I'd repeated it to myself and to everyone who would listen so many times that the idea was etched into my brain. How could I change it? It was as if it was a part of me. Like an ingrained belief, and everyone knew those were very hard to change.

"Branthor," she whispered.

I opened my eyes and instantly lost myself in hers.

"I just want to know what it feels like," she said. "To belong to the one who was meant for me. And if it's only for tonight, then I'm okay with that."

"Are you sure?"

"Yes."

I opened the bottle, poured oil into my palm, then said to her, "Lie back."

Teal

His big, rough hands on my body had me burning with desire. He rubbed the oil into every inch of my exposed skin, starting from my neck, down my shoulders and arms. He massaged my tense muscles until I was putty in his hands. I wasn't sure this was how the oil was supposed to be used, but I wasn't going to complain. I wanted Branthor to touch me everywhere. All at once, if possible.

His hands traveled up my arms and down my chest. He rubbed the oil between the peaks of my breasts, then around them, intentionally avoiding them for a few minutes. My nipples were so hard that they almost felt painful. I was turned on like I'd never been in my life, and my pussy was gushing for him already. The need for him was so intense that my core started to hurt.

"You're so beautiful," he whispered.

"You've seen me naked twice," I said. "When is it my turn?"

"Patience."

He wasn't in a hurry, and I liked that. At the same time, though, I needed him to do more. Much more. My hands reached for one of his wrists, and I tried guiding him towards my breast. He resisted me for a moment, but when I groaned in frustration, he finally complied. He cupped my breasts with both his hands, squeezing and kneading lightly. I arched my back into his touch and bit my lip.

"Please," I murmured.

He touched my nipples with his fingers, so lightly that it was barely a tease.

"Branthor, you're barely brushing my skin," I complained.

"I'm afraid I might hurt you," he said.

I glared at him. "This again? I know I look frail, but trust me, I'm not."

"Yes, you are. I'm not taking any risks."

I let out an "ugh!" so he knew how much I disagreed with him. He added a little more pressure, but it still wasn't enough. He moved his hands down my stomach, then down my sides. He covered me in oil thoroughly, and it was all so slippery and delicious. He stopped above my pelvis and shifted his position so he could reach my feet.

He started with my soles and moved up to my ankles and calves, massaging me slowly, in circles. I admitted I loved the attention. The way he was looking at me as he diligently explored my body was enough to start another fire inside me, this time deep into my soul. The fire in my pussy was one thing – needy and desperate – but the fire in my soul was different – hopeful and all-consuming. I could tell that this man wanted me, and not just for my body.

His hands moved up my thighs. He kneaded my inner thighs, and I instinctively opened my legs for him. His breath hitched, and he froze for a few seconds. His deep green eyes were focused on my pussy. I spread my legs a little more, and he didn't protest. I wanted him to have the best view; maybe then he'd start moving a little faster.

"You don't know what you're doing to me," he whispered huskily.

"I think I have a pretty good idea," I chuckled.

I nudged him with my foot lightly, and he resumed massaging me. Slowly, he bent over me, closer and closer.

"May I taste you?"

I felt myself blush to the tips of my ears. My whole skin was on fire.

"Yes."

It was sexy that he wanted my consent, but at the same time... when he asked questions like that, I was in serious danger of losing my voice.

He nodded and climbed on the bed, settling between my legs. He gently placed his big hands underneath my buttocks and lifted me up to his mouth. First, he inhaled deeply, and I thought I was going to faint. It was a little embarrassing, but at the same time, so sinfully good. Then I felt the tip of his tongue on my pussy, and I let out a mewl without meaning to.

He started slow, exploring my folds with only the tip of his tongue, then dipping between them to lick the juice pouring out of me. He licked my entrance, but didn't dive right in, wanting to savor every second. His tongue traced a line to my clit, and a jolt went through me, making my body tremble.

When he flattened his tongue against me, covering me from my clit to my entrance, I let out a cry and grabbed the sheets. Of course his tongue was big enough to cover that entire part of me. He licked me like that for a while, almost sending me into a frenzy. It was incredible, but not enough. There was something building inside me, and I felt like the culmination of it was just around the corner, but at the same time, so far away.

He focused his attention on my clit alone, flicking it with the tip of his tongue, slowly at first, then faster, and before I knew what was happening, my back was arching, my toes were curling, and an orgasm crashed through me so hard that it almost separated my soul from my body. Or so it felt. I was dazed for a few seconds, not realizing I was practically screaming.

Branthor slowed down, allowing me to ride the waves of pleasure. When I opened my eyes, my vision was blurry. I stared at the ceiling until I could see clearly again, then my hands reached down, and my fingers sank into his long, soft hair. He stopped then and lifted himself up to look at me.

Our eyes met. It felt like I was swimming in a warm pond. I felt so light that it was as if I was one with the water.

"You're the best thing I've ever tasted," he said.

My lips parted and closed. I swallowed heavily. Before I could find my voice, he sat up and started removing his clothes. I watched him in awe, my gaze taking in his wide chest, the hair that covered it, his strong abs, and the massive cock that sprung out of his pants as he removed them.

Okay. Wow! Okay.

I swallowed heavily, feeling my heart thundering in my chest. This was too much. His cock was bigger than my arm, and definitely thicker. There was no way – no way! – that it would fit without splitting me in two, even with the magical oil from the Temple.

What was the oil doing, anyway? I focused on my body, on the parts that Branthor had rubbed, and discovered that it felt oddly tingling. It had a soothing effect, but was that enough to help me… take him?

And the worst part was that my voice was gone. Not that I wanted him to stop, but I was just so stunned that not even my thoughts were as coherent anymore. I was completely overwhelmed by him.

"We don't have to go all the way," he said.

I blinked at him, not quite understanding what he was saying. Then it dawned on me that he was ready to stop if I gave as much as a sign that I wasn't sure about this, and I quickly shook my head.

"Are you sure, Teal?"

I nodded vigorously, wishing my voice would return soon, so I could tell him that I still wanted him, even after seeing what he was packing. I needed him to be the one to take my virginity. I didn't care what happened the next day, I just knew this was right.

"I will get you ready," he said, and poured more oil into his palm.

As he started rubbing the oil on my pussy, he leaned in and took my left breast into his mouth. My entire breast. He sucked on it and rolled his tongue around it, then moved to the other. I knew my breasts were rather small, but to him... they were tiny. He could probably fit them both in his mouth if he tried a little.

The things he was doing with his mouth distracted me from what he was doing with his hand. Until he slipped a finger inside me, and I tensed up.

"Shh..." He whispered. "I'll go slowly. I will give you as much time as you need. And if you want me to stop, just let me know."

Needing to hold on to something as he fingered me lazily, I grabbed onto his hair again, pulling slightly at the roots. He let out a groan but didn't push me away. I realized that he liked it. Maybe it turned him on, even.

"Kiss me," I said. Oh, good. My voice was back. And so needy that I barely recognized myself. I hadn't known I could sound like this.

He aligned his head with mine, and my fingers moved into his beard. It was so long and soft... I loved it. Who would've thought I loved bearded, hairy men? Our lips met, and I moaned into the kiss. I could feel his finger explore my pussy, stretching it slowly, gently. At the same time, his tongue battled with mine, not that I stood a chance. It was hard for me to keep up with him, and I just gave up and let him explore my mouth as he pleased.

"Everything about you is delicious," he whispered. "Intoxicating. I can't get enough of you, Teal."

That was a good thing, right? It meant he might not want to take me to the Temple tomorrow. But that was not why I wanted to sleep with him.

Sure, I hoped this would solidify the bond between us, making it impossible for him to ever say again that he didn't want me as his bride. But at the same time, I just wanted to do it, no matter the consequences.

Consequences that... if this didn't work out... I refused to think about.

He started moving his finger a little faster, in and out, in and out, and whatever pain I'd felt when he'd first penetrated me was gone. He curled his finger slightly, and I arched my back, my eyes growing wide. He'd hit a spot inside me that almost had me see stars.

"Again," I panted. "Do that again."

He grinned and did as I asked. He hit that spot again and again, rubbing it, teasing it, until my body went rigid, and I came again, harder and longer than the first time. My pussy gushed, and the juices spilled out of me and onto his hand. He didn't stop, though, didn't give me a chance to recover. He added a second finger and stretched me even more. This time, there was no pain. It was as if my pussy was stretching for him at the smallest invitation.

He fucked me with two fingers until I was a writhing mess again, screaming my third release. I was tired already, but I knew I had to keep up with the pleasure he was offering me.

"I need you inside me," I said. "Please, now. I can't take it anymore. It's too much..."

"If this is too much..."

"Branthor, you know what I mean. Please."

"I'm not sure you're ready yet."

"I am."

He pulled his fingers out of me, and I instantly felt the emptiness he left behind. I squirmed and wiggled my hips as he poured more oil into his palm, then started spreading it thoroughly all over his huge cock. I stopped moving and watched, mesmerized.

The impressive length glistened with oil, but also with his precum. The mushroom head was big and dark pink, and as stretched as I was, my mind couldn't wrap around the possibility of it fitting inside me. He rubbed the oil for a few minutes, and I shamelessly watched him. I barely blinked, not wanting to miss anything. He groaned as he stroked himself, faster and faster. I saw how more precum seeped out of his slit, and I licked my lips. Would he let me taste him if I asked?

His hand stopped at the base of his cock, and he squeezed rather harshly. He let out a deep, primal growl, then leaned over me, pushing my legs apart. But there was something wrong with the position. He couldn't quite reach me, since I was so small, and he was so big. He frowned, then grabbed a pillow and put it under my lower back, effectively elevating my pelvis. Now we were more aligned.

"If you want me to stop..." As he said that, he rubbed the tip of his cock against my entrance.

"No." My pussy was already throbbing for him, ready to suck him in. "I'm ready. Please do it."

He nodded and started thrusting inside me, slowly, carefully, his eyes never looking away from my face. He studied every little expression I made, listened to every sound that left my lips. But it was all okay because there was no pain. It was mind-blowing how well the oil had worked. My body stretched for him, and as he entered me inch by inch, I felt full, but not like I was going to break. On the contrary, I felt like whatever he could give me, I could take.

"Does it hurt?"

I shook my head. "Not at all. What's in the oil?"

He chuckled. "I have no idea."

"Maybe it's a secret recipe," I said.

"It doesn't matter, as long as it works," he said.

"Oh, it works."

He continued penetrating me, little by little, until he was completely sheathed. He stopped then, and looked down at the place where we were connected. I looked too, and my eyes nearly popped out of my head when I saw how deeply he was buried inside me and how stretched I was around him. The most shocking thing was that I could see the shape of his massive cock along my stomach. Somehow, it didn't hurt. It was as if my pussy had adapted to his size.

"Move," I said, wanting to see with my own eyes how his cock pumped in and out of me.

"Teal," he breathed. "It's so hard for me to hold back."

"Don't hold back, then."

"I must. I could hurt you. Badly."

"Don't think about that. See? The oil works."

"Yes, but the strength that I possess..."

I placed my hand on his cheek. "Just... do your best... But do something. All I can think about is how I want you to..." I bit my lip. "I want you to..."

"What?" He caressed my hair with his fingers.

"How much I want you to fill me with your seed."

I couldn't believe I'd just said that. I was supposed to be a virgin! Innocent. Well, not anymore.

"If you keep talking like that," he growled, "This won't last more than sixty seconds."

I laughed. "As long as we both have fun..."

He started pulling out of me, inch by inch, and stopped only when the tip was in. I watched in amazement how his cock moved through my body. And it felt incredible. I felt so full, but in a pleasant, satisfying way. He pushed back in, just as slowly, and all my nerves trembled with pleasure.

"Please tell me you intend to move faster than this," I said.

"I don't want to risk—"

"Hurting me," I cut him off. "You're not. You won't. This feels... amazing. I never want it to stop."

He pursed his lips, took a deep breath, pulled out again as he released it, and pushed back in, faster and harder than before. I let out a long moan and held onto his shoulders. Seeing how I gave no sign of pain, he did it again and again, increasing the pace with each thrust.

That literally turned me into a puddle. Complete goo. The sensations I felt through my body were overwhelming. My brain couldn't keep up with them, couldn't interpret them fully. All I knew was that I wanted more, more... until I was going to burst.

Oh, I was so close... so close... When it happened, my vision went dark for a second. I came so hard that my entire body shook with the force of the orgasm, and I cried out so loud that I was certain the whole of Mossdale could hear me. I couldn't stop, though. I couldn't hold it in. My orgasm was like crashing waves. Over and over, and I realized it wasn't just one orgasm, there were many. I kept coming until I couldn't physically withstand it anymore, and I collapsed, motionless.

Branthor thrust a few more times before he finally stilled. I felt his hot cum shoot inside me, deep into my womb – I wasn't even sure where exactly my womb was positioned in my body – until a bulge formed there, like a pocket meant to hold his cum.

I barely had the strength to look down when I felt him fill me to the brim.

"Teal," he whispered. "I... I never thought it would feel this way."

I opened my mouth to say something, but nothing came out. I was stunned and exhausted.

He gave another grunt, and I felt one last rush of cum fill me, before he leaned onto his side and slowly pulled out of me. The instant he was out, my pussy gushed with his seed. It spilled out of me, white, hot, and thick. The sheets were ruined.

Branthor collapsed next to me. I realized he was just as spent as I was. For minutes, we lay there, breathing heavily, trying to wrap our heads around what we'd just done.

"I never thought it would feel like this either," I said. If this was what sex was, then I wanted to have it every night. With him. I just hoped my pussy could take it. Even with the oil, it felt like a mighty task.

He gathered me in his arms and pulled me close to his chest. More of his seed spilled onto the bed when I moved. I cringed for a second, then thought I'd better get used to it. It was going to happen every time.

Now, the question was... Did he want to do it again with me? Every night for as long as we lived?

The real, most pressing question was... Had he changed his mind about me? I thought of asking him, but I was so spent that I didn't think I could hold a conversation, especially one as serious as this. It would have to wait.

For now, I needed sleep.

BRANTHOR

I watched her sleep for most of the night. I was tired myself but watching her was more important than getting the rest I needed. Now that I'd been inside her and filled her with my seed, I couldn't let go of her. Not only for a minute. She was mine.

My bride. Teal. The bride I'd never wanted.

Well, she was here now, and I knew I couldn't let her leave. I'd said over and over that I was going to take her back to the Temple, up to the moment when I slipped into her body, and it was increasingly clear to me that it had been a lie.

I couldn't take her back. She was mine, meant for me. It was ridiculous to keep fighting this. It was fate.

Before dawn, I carefully got out of bed. She murmured in her sleep, turned on the other side, and I tucked her in. On my tiptoes, I went to take a shower. I'd never been so careful and silent in my own house. With Teal here, I noticed how I was starting to adapt and change my habits. I washed myself, brushed my long hair and my beard, put on fresh clothes, and went to make breakfast. As I passed through the living room, I saw the marriage contract on the table. Kairos had left it.

My brother had signed in my stead, but it was not enough. For the marriage to be truly official, I had to sign it, and then take it to the Temple, or send someone. I smiled as I leafed through it and reached for a pen. But as the tip of the pen met the paper, I stopped. What if I waited for Teal to wake up, and I signed it in her presence? I wanted to see her face when I did it. So, I placed it back on the table and went into the kitchen.

I heard Teal wake up and go to the bathroom as I was frying eggs. I made freshly squeezed carrot and apple juice, placed our breakfast on a tray, and brought it into the living room. When Teal emerged wearing a beautiful blue dress – one of Nova's – everything was ready. I was waiting for her with the contract in my hand.

"Good morning," she said.

"Good morning. How did you sleep?"

"Great!" Then she moved towards me, and I noticed she was wobbling a bit, as if she wasn't sure how to use her legs. "Ugh! You know, what we did last night was amazing, but I think the oil's effects are wearing off."

My eyes widened, and I was instantly by her side, helping her the last few steps to the couch.

"I can rub some on you again," I said. "Maybe it will help."

She winced. "Yes, we should do that." Her stomach rumbled, and she chuckled awkwardly. "Food first. I'm starving."

I sat down next to her and showed her the contract. "How about we do this first, and then eat?"

"What is that?" Just as she asked, she realized what I was holding. Her eyes widened, and then her lips curved into a smile. "Are you going to..."

"Sign it? Yes. I'm making this official."

"Branthor..."

"Teal, you are my wife. That is, if you still want me as your husband."

"Yes!"

She jumped to her feet and launched herself at me. She clung to my neck, hiding her face in my hair, whispering in my ear.

"I knew it," she said. "I knew you would change your mind after last night."

My blood went cold. I gently pushed her away, and she slipped off me and back onto the couch. She reached for the food on the table, beginning to pile it onto a plate.

"What do you mean?" I said.

"What?" She looked at me with innocent eyes as she munched on a strip of fried bacon.

"You knew I would change my mind after last night. That's what you said."

"Um... yes?"

"Does that mean you planned it? You slept with me to convince me to let you stay?"

"What?" She swallowed heavily, coughed, and took a sip of juice. Her face went slightly pale. Paler than it usually was.

I pushed the contract away from me.

"Branthor." She whispered my name carefully.

"Teal, did you do it to manipulate me?

"What?!"

"You did, didn't you? You didn't have sex with me because you wanted it, because the attraction between us was too much to bear, but because you knew it would bind us, form a connection that even I, in my selfishness, couldn't deny."

"What are you talking about? Branthor, of course not. Yes, I want to stay. Yes, I want to be your wife and build a life with you, but I would never manipulate you into it. Every time you said you were taking me back to the Temple, I didn't argue with you. Even last night, I told you that I didn't care about the consequences."

I sat up abruptly. "Because you knew there would be no consequences."

She sat up too, matching my energy, which was impressive given how small she was. "I don't like the way you're talking to me right now," she said. "I don't appreciate you accusing me of manipulation. I had sex with you because I wanted to."

With that, she stomped away.

"Where are you going?" I asked.

"Nowhere!" She kept stomping towards the front door.

"Teal!"

"I need some air. Don't follow me."

With a grunt, she opened the door and slammed it closed behind her. It was no easy feat since the door was grendel sized.

I stood there, stunned. Teal had just walked out on me.

It was my fault. What was I thinking accusing her of something so awful? And what did it matter, anyway? I still wasn't going to take her back to the Temple. My fate had been sealed the moment she'd jumped out of my birthday cake.

"I'm such an idiot," I muttered to myself.

I wanted to go after her, but what if it upset her even more? She'd said she needed some air. She was probably on her way to Nova's house to complain about me. For now, I was going to give her space. I was sure she would come back soon enough, after she calmed down, and by then, I'd have a decent apology prepared.

I'd messed up. I had to say "sorry" and mean it.

TEAL

I didn't know where I was going. I just wanted out of there, so I could breathe and be alone with my thoughts for a minute. Mossdale was bustling with activity, and every time someone recognized me, they wanted to stop and chat. They were lovely people – the grendels, their wives, and their hybrid children – but right now, I needed space. I was the latest addition to their community, and that made me interesting. They were curious about who I was, where I came from, and if I liked it here.

How could I tell them that I couldn't stay? That Branthor wouldn't sign the marriage contract and make us a real couple? Husband and wife. They were so happy for us, and I couldn't utter a word about what had just happened today.

Branthor thought I'd slept with him to manipulate him. So what if I'd hoped it would change his mind? It was only natural. But that didn't mean I'd done it to manipulate him. For him to say that to me was simply disrespectful. Now I was wondering myself if staying in Mossdale as his bride really was a good idea.

After all that had happened between us, he didn't seem to want me badly enough. Then why did I still want him?

In my attempt to avoid the people of Mossdale, I left the main road and snuck behind the houses. The fences were so tall that no one could see me from their backyards. I didn't know this part of the town at all, but I could see the mountains rising behind the houses, and the woods. All I wanted was to be alone in nature.

I walked and walked, until the houses were far behind me. I turned south and walked along the tree line. When the trees became sparse and the terrain rocky, I slowed down and allowed myself to breathe more mindfully. It was quiet out here. I found a wide rock, so wide that I could lie on it, and I did just that. With my face towards the sky, I watched the birds fly high overhead and listened to the sounds of the mountains.

This place was beautiful. To me, it was special. I'd never traveled outside the city of Fortitude, which was surrounded by protective walls. The nature there didn't compare to what lay before me here. The air was so fresh and crisp that it almost hurt to breathe it. Maybe because I was used to the polluted air of Fortitude. The air in Mossdale was too strong for me.

After a few minutes, I stretched like a big, lazy cat. Turning onto my stomach, I looked at the mountains above. Their peaks shot up to the sky. I noticed a dark spot in the rocky side of the mountain, and I stood up, curiosity getting the better of me.

"Is that..." I walked over there, and the closer I got, the bigger the dark spot became. "No..."

It turned out to be exactly why I'd expected. It was the mouth of a cave. I wondered if these were the Thundering Caves Branthor had told me about. He hadn't mentioned any other caves in the area. He'd told me this was his favorite place, and when he had nothing else to do, he'd take his equipment and explore the caverns, hoping to find things no one had found before.

I knew it was a bad idea to go in by myself. I stopped at the mouth of the cave, which was huge, and looked inside. From a distance, it had looked completely black, but from up close, the sunlight reached pretty far inside. The cool, humid air beckoned to me.

"I won't go far," I told myself.

And I wasn't going to. I just wanted to be in this space that Branthor loved so much, absorb its energy, and hope the stalactites and stalagmites revealed to me secrets about the man I loved. Maybe they would whisper in my ear something I didn't know, something I could use to convince him we were meant to be together, and it was ridiculous to fight it.

The floor of the cave was made of shiny, slippery rock. There was water trickling between the cracks, and I had to be careful where I stepped. I used the rock formations for support, and I advanced until it was too dark to see ahead. I stopped, found a place to sit down, and spent a few peaceful moments there. Compared to the beautiful weather outside, it was chilly in here. It was a good thing my dress was long. I wrapped the skirt around my feet and hugged my knees to my chest.

"Are you going to tell me his secrets?" I spoke to the cave walls. All they did was send my voice deeper into the many caverns. It echoed far inside the mountain. No one answered. I chuckled. "Why am I being so silly?"

I knew why. I was sad. Disappointed. And I really didn't want to go back to the real world. I loved it here. I wanted to stay. But I also didn't want to be with Branthor if he was just going to keep accusing me of manipulating him. As if a tiny thing like me could manipulate a massive grendel like him.

I stayed in the cave for what felt like an hour, maybe more. I was starting to feel cold, but I liked it here. My thoughts settled down after a while, and so did my emotions. At some point, I noticed that I felt better, and I was ready to return to civilization, so to speak. I got up, and as I found my way out, I ran my fingers over the walls and rock formations, as if wanting to absorb everything this place was willing to share with me. I understood why Branthor loved it so much. There was something about it... Something mystical. I couldn't explain it.

As I emerged from the cave, it must have been past noon. The sky had turned cloudy, and the sun was hiding. I looked towards the small town of Mossdale, safely nestled in the valley below, and a sense of longing rose inside me.

This was home. I'd only been here for two days, but I could feel it in my body and in my soul. Home. I couldn't give up so easily. I'd waited five years to find my purpose, my place in this world that had been bent on proving to me that it didn't want me since the day I was born. And now I was here, and I had a real chance at happiness.

Branthor was being an idiot, which was not unheard of when it came to men. As a woman, I had to be smart. Smarter than him. He'd upset me earlier today, but I was past it. Now that I'd calmed down, I was certain we could work it out.

I smiled to myself and started on the way back. I was lost in thought, and when I heard a branch snap to my right, I ignored it. The forest was teeming with critters. Another branch snapped, and I ignored that one, too. This was their home, not mine. But then there were footsteps, heavy and determined, and before I realized that they were moving towards me, it was too late.

Someone grabbed me from behind. It was a man, strong enough to crush me if he wanted to, but not a grendel. He was human. I could tell by the size of his hand as it pressed against my mouth so I wouldn't scream.

Another man emerged from behind a tree.

"Did you think you would get rid of us so easily, little sister?"

My brothers.

I tried to scream, kick, but it was no use. They shoved a dirty rag into my mouth and covered my head with a stinky bag made of rough fabric. Then one of them grabbed me from underneath my arms, the other grabbed my legs, and they carried me away. No matter how hard I struggled, they weren't impressed. Compared to me, they were tall, big, and muscular. I was the only one in our family who'd inherited our mother's frail bone structure.

"Calm down," my brother said. "You'll be back home with us soon enough."

"We couldn't abandon you with the giants, Teal. You're our sister, and we love you."

Sister. Right. I was their slave, and they needed me. A few days without me cooking, cleaning, and doing laundry for them, and here they were, kidnapping me. I wondered where our father was. Was he waiting for us at home? Had he ordered this?

Branthor. I thought of Branthor. I willed my emotions to reach him, call to him. But he was mad at me. He was probably still thinking about last night, confused as to whether it had been real or manipulation. He hadn't run after me when I left. He hadn't followed me. I'd spent hours in the mountains and in his favorite cave, and he hadn't come.

This was it. It was over. Branthor wasn't coming at all.

Branthor

Teal had been gone too long. I waited an hour, then went looking for her, first at Nova's house, then at Holly's and Maren's. No one had seen her. Panic settled in quickly, and I felt paralyzed. Helpless. Before I knew it, I was out on the roads and alleys of Mossdale, looking for her, asking everyone if they'd seen her.

A few people told me they'd seen her hours ago, and she'd seemed agitated and eager to be alone. They hadn't found her as chatty as she usually was, and they asked me if something was wrong.

How could I tell them? I couldn't.

How could I tell them that it was all my fault, and I was the biggest idiot alive? After she'd left, I'd realized how much I'd hurt her. Accusing her like that... What was I thinking?

As usual, I'd only been concerned with myself. In my selfishness, I'd hurt her feelings and literally chased her away. I'd made it impossible for her to be in the same room as me.

Someone told me they'd last seen her heading towards the mountains, outside of Mossdale. I wondered why she'd go alone in the wilderness. It wasn't exactly safe out there. There were wild animals, and even if it was the middle of the day, it wasn't a good idea for a small thing like her to go exploring on her own. I guessed she'd needed space to think, and the grendels and wives of Mossdale could be quite nosey, especially since she was new in town. They were all curious about her, and they weren't hiding it very well. Okay, they weren't hiding it at all.

I was pretty sure they'd scared Teal away with their endless questions.

I'd scared her away.

I looked for her left and right. It took me a while to notice the little clues she'd left behind – like a broken twig, and the imprint of her shoe on a soft patch of soil. Most of the terrain here was rocky, and I had to track her carefully. There weren't many signs I could use to find her. I got closer and closer to the Thundering Caves. No. She couldn't have gone in there. She was smart enough to know it wasn't safe.

I'd told her about the caves and about how deep they went. Plus, beyond a certain point, it was impossible to explore without a flashlight.

I increased my pace and stopped at the mouth of the cave. The sun was in the clouds, and I squinted to see inside. I opened my mouth to call her name, but then, from the corner of my eye, I saw something weird.

There was a patch of grass that was flattened out, as if there had been a struggle there. There were footprints too, and I recognized the imprint of Teal's small shoe. Her feet were so tiny that I was impressed they made shoes her size. The other footprints were foreign to me, and they looked much bigger than hers.

"Two men," I said as I started tracking them. "Human males."

Along the years, very few human males had stepped foot in Mossdale. They had no reason to be here. This was suspicious, to say the least. A lump formed in my throat when I saw that while their footprints continued, Teal's had disappeared.

"What happened here?"

Teal would've never left with two strangers. She'd tried to fight them off, I was sure, but she was just too tiny and weak.

I increased my pace just as the sun peeked out from behind the clouds. It was a lovely day, but inside my soul, a thunderstorm roared. If something bad happened to Teal, it would be my fault. She'd left the house because of me. I'd upset her with my ridiculous accusations, and now I was going to lose her forever.

I followed the tracks deep into the woods, then down the mountain. I walked as fast as I could, my heavy footsteps making the earth shake as I barreled through the trees. I could tell I was getting close when the signs I tracked became more obvious. The men knew I was onto them, and they were moving faster, breaking twigs and branches in the process. Soon enough, I heard them up ahead.

"Hey! Stop!" I yelled at them, and at the same time, broke into a run. "I said stop!"

My voice thundered through the forest. I emerged into a clearing, and there they were. Two young men in uniform. They'd thrown Teal to the side, and she was struggling on the ground. As they pulled out guns, she managed to remove the bag they'd covered her head with, and the makeshift gag they'd used to silence her.

"Branthor!"

The men eyed me with reinforced interest. And anger. Before I could make a move, they shot at me with their rifles. The bullets bit into my flesh, but that only served to enrage me. I let out a growl and barreled towards them. They shot me again and again, but that didn't stop me. Yes, I felt the bullets, but they were nothing compared to what they'd done to my bride. They'd put a bag over her head and kidnapped her. I didn't even care who they were. I recognized the uniform of the Peacemakers, but they had no power here. The Peacemakers policed the humans, not the monsters.

When I was close enough, they still thought they could bring me down with their ridiculous firearms. I grabbed their rifles and bent them with my bare hands. They looked at me with wide, incredulous eyes, then finally, they had the bright idea to start running.

Too bad they were only human, and their short, pathetic legs could only get them so far before I closed the space between us and grabbed them both by their shirts. They screamed in fear.

"Put me down," one of them said. "We are family! What are you doing? We are Teal's brothers."

"She's our sister," the other one screamed.

That made me see red. They were here to kidnap their own sister? What sort of family was this? In my rage, I threw one against a tree, and the other against a rock. Something cracked. Maybe an arm or a leg. I was ready to grab them again and throw them, maybe break a few more bones.

"Stop!" Teal came running from behind. She clung to my arm, trying to hold me back. "Stop, please. They're telling the truth. They're my brothers."

I looked at her, confused. "Your brothers kidnapped you and shot at me. I don't understand."

She swallowed heavily. "I... I didn't want you to know."

"Know what?"

"That they're..." She was struggling to find her words. "They've always been abusive. And controlling. Them and my father. I cooked for them, cleaned for them, did everything around the house. Since my mother died five years ago, I was their maid.

When I got the letter from the Temple, we had a huge fight, and when I left the next day, they didn't even let me take a few clothes with me."

"What?!" I was appalled at what I was hearing. "Teal, these are not men. These are monsters. And they certainly aren't your family. Your family is supposed to love and cherish you. And keep you safe."

She smiled weakly. "I know. You are my family. You, and Kairos, Ragnar, Orion, Nova, Holly, Maren, Maverick, Coral, and Pearl." She looked at me, hope glimmering in her eyes. "And Holly's baby, of course," she added with a smile. "All of you. All of Mossdale. I haven't felt so welcomed and wanted in my life."

The two men – Teal's brothers – groaned and started crawling away from us. They were badly hurt, and frankly, I'd barely even touched them.

I took a step towards them, but Teal held me back.

"Let them go," she said. "I think they learned their lesson."

One of them turned to look over his shoulder. He was struggling to stand up.

"Don't," he panted, his eyes wide with horror. "Don't hurt us. We're leaving."

"Do you intend to come back with reinforcements?" I asked.

"No," said the other. "No, never."

"Good. Because next time, it won't just be me. I'll invite my brothers to the party, and unlike you two, they happen to adore Teal. I won't have to tear you limb from limb, because they will."

They scrambled towards each other, so they could lean on each other and run further down the slope. They advanced slowly, both hurt, both in pain. It was hard to let them escape with their lives.

"Thank you," Teal said.

I turned to her and touched her face with the tips of my fingers, careful not to hurt her like they'd had.

"Are you okay?"

"Yes, now I am. It's a good thing you showed up. I'm sure they have a van somewhere."

"If they do, it's a long way to it. These roads are impossible. That's why we have a portal."

Teal looked around us, at the trees I'd almost torn down in my blind rage. She shuddered. I pulled her into my arms, and she rested her head against my hip.

"You came after me," she said. "I thought you were upset."

"I was stupid, not upset. You, on the other hand, have every right to be mad at me."

"Not anymore. I spent some time in your favorite place, the Thundering Caves, and I realized I can't be mad at you."

"Teal..."

"Shh... let me finish." She pulled away and craned her neck to look into my eyes. "I can't be mad at you because I–"

"Love you," I cut her off. "I love you, Teal."

She stared at me, then laughed. "You couldn't let me say it first."

"No way."

She laughed again, then whispered. "I love you too, Branthor."

She lifted herself on her tiptoes, and I bent to meet her halfway. Before we could kiss, I let out a grunt. I was in pain. I was just realizing now, as the adrenaline was slowly leaving my body. After all, I'd been shot quite a few times.

"Are you okay?"

"Just a few scratches." I winced. They might've looked like scratches on my huge body, but they were wounds, and some of them were deep, and the bullets were still inside.

"We should go back," she said. "Now, before it gets worse. Can you walk?"

"Yes."

She let out a breath of relief. "Good. Because believe it or not, I can't carry you."

I laughed and instantly regretted it.

It hurt.

But Teal was safe, and that was all that mattered.

Teal

Branthor took a few steps and fell to one knee. He was so heavy that when his knee connected with the ground, I swore there was a small quake. I was quick to move out of the way, then rushed back to his side.

"Are you okay? What if you stay here, and I go and call for help?"

"No," he protested. "We're far from home, and the thought of you wandering alone through the wilderness is unbearable." He clenched his jaw and made an effort to stand up. "I can do this, don't worry about me. I'm tough."

I chuckled. "I know you are."

I felt so bad that I could do nothing to help him. He was huge, and my small frame couldn't even help him stand. He couldn't lean on me for support. On the contrary, I had to be careful in case he collapsed again. Because if he couldn't control his movements, he could easily crush me, and the last thing we needed was for this day to end in a horror show.

We advanced slowly. We had no water, and I hadn't eaten anything since the night before, which wasn't ideal. I was feeling hungry, thirsty, and tired. But I couldn't rush Branthor. He was bleeding all over. It seemed to me like he was unaware that he was covered in wounds. My brothers had shot him too many times for me to be able to count. Anyone would've been dead. But not Branthor. Not a grendel.

"This is all my fault," he said.

"Not true," I hurried to reassure him.

"Yes, it is true. You ran away because of me."

"I didn't run away," I said. "I just needed some air, and the town felt a little suffocating. Don't get me wrong, I love everyone, but I wanted to find a peaceful spot where I could think. I came across the Thundering Caves by accident, and remembered you said it's your favorite place. I went inside and spent an hour just thinking. It was amazing. I see why you like the caves so much."

"Your brothers caught you as you were coming out."

"Yes. And that's not your fault, Branthor. It's theirs."

We walked in silence for a few minutes, but I could tell there was more on his mind.

"Why didn't you tell me about them?" he asked. "Why didn't you tell me how awful they are?"

I shrugged. "I was embarrassed, I guess. And it didn't matter anymore. I was here, with you, far away from my family. I didn't think for a second that they would come for me. The Marriage Temple is clear in its rules. Once a bride is bound to her husband through the mating ceremony, she belongs to him, and the bride's family has no claim over her. Both my brothers, and my father, are Peacemakers. They've been the law for so long that they got used to getting what they want."

"But if I were to take you back to the Temple..." he said, his voice shaking.

"No," I stopped him. "Let's not talk about that. Not now. Now, we must focus on putting one foot in front of the other. You're bleeding, Branthor, and you're becoming increasingly weak. We must get to Mossdale."

He shook his head. "I'm sorry, Teal. I'm so sorry. I was an idiot."

I smiled. "Yes, you were. Still are a bit of an idiot. But you're my idiot."

"I don't deserve you."

"Right now, I think I'll have to agree with you." I smiled at him. His eyes crinkled at the corners when he smiled back. "You did save me, though. You came looking for me, and that's what matters."

"Do you think you might forgive me one day?" he asked.

"Hm... I'll think about it. I'll let you know."

He chuckled, then groaned in pain. "Yes, you do that. Let me know."

I held his hand as we walked together. I could see the houses of Mossdale in the distance. We were nearly there. Unfortunately, Branthor was even slower, and we had to stop many times so he could rest.

"We're close now," I said. "Please, just wait here and let me go get help. I know my way from here."

Branthor scanned the valley below. I would have to cross a wide, open terrain to get to the first houses, but it was no big deal, and it wasn't dangerous at all. My brothers were long gone. I knew they weren't going to come back, but I also knew Branthor wasn't convinced. He didn't know them. Behind their stupid bravado, my brothers were cowards. They were also too proud to try something again and be defeated again. They also cared more about their lives than taking me back home to be their slave.

One day, they would get married. Now that I wasn't around anymore, sooner rather than later. I felt sorry for their future wives. I knew I couldn't do anything about it. I'd served my time, so to speak, paid for any bad karma I might've had. It was time to move on and stop thinking about the past.

"Okay, Teal," Branthor finally conceded. "But be careful."

"I will." I helped him sit down. "Don't move. I'll bring your brothers."

"Teal." He gently took me by the arm and pulled me close to him. "I just wanted to say... You are my mate. I will sign the marriage contract as soon as I get to Mossdale."

I lifted myself on my tiptoes and placed my hand on his hairy cheek. Even with him sitting down, I was still too short, and he was too tall.

"I know you will," I said. "I am your bride, and you're my husband. A grumpy husband, but alas, these were the cards I was dealt."

He chuckled and leaned in to place a kiss on my lips. I closed my eyes and clung to him, pulling him closer, wanting to feel his strong body against mine. We kissed, but at some point, he winced, and I moved away and realized I'd accidentally touched one of the bullet wounds.

"I have to go," I said. "You're getting worse. The wounds could get infected."

"I will be fine, my love. Now that I have you, I will be fine."

I smiled. "Don't move. I'll be back in no time."

I turned on my heel and started running towards the houses in the distance. My feet ached, but I ignored them. A few more things in my body hurt from when my brothers had grabbed me, but I was sure it was nothing. Maybe a few bruises on my ribs, arms, and legs. They would fade in a few days, and then there would be no more bruises on my body. Not ever.

I made my way into Mossdale and went straight to Orion's house. It was the closest. I banged on the door, and his daughter Coral answered.

"Are your parents at home?" I asked.

She looked at me with wide eyes. She was as tall as me, even though she was only six years old.

"Yes," she said. "In the backyard."

She let me in, and as soon as I saw Maren, I ran into her arms. I started sobbing, and it just dawned on me how scared I'd been all this time, since my brothers had grabbed me and shot Branthor.

"Quick," I said. "He needs help. He's hurt, and he can barely walk."

They didn't wait for me to explain myself. Orion rushed through the house and out the front door to get his brothers. Maren and I followed, though it was difficult for us to keep up with them. Nova joined us. Holly stayed home, though it took some convincing.

As exhausted as I was, I ran as fast as I could to show them where I'd left Branthor. On the way there, I told them about what had happened. Fortunately, they didn't ask me too many questions about my abusive family. For now, there were more important things to worry about. But I knew the questions would come soon, in the following days.

We found Branthor on his side, with his eyes closed and one hand clutching his chest. Through his fingers, dark blood seeped into the ground.

Kairos, Ragnar, and Orion had to carry him. Now that they were in charge, I could slow down. My feet were killing me. I was glad Nova and Maren were there with me, allowing me to lean on them.

"It's going to be okay," Maren said.

"She's right," Nova said. "Come on. You need water, food, and a hot bath. We'll take care of you, Teal."

"Thank you."

"We're sisters," Maren said.

And I believed them. I was so blessed to finally have sisters!

Branthor

I didn't want to think that the bullet wounds were a big deal, but it turned out... they were. When my brothers found me, I was barely holding on to consciousness. They carried me in their arms, all the way home, where they deposited me on the couch. Teal, Maren, and Nova rushed to find pillows and blankets, so I could be more comfortable.

The next step was to bring the old grendel females, Sava and Varna. They had knowledge about plant medicine. Unfortunately, they said neither of them was equipped to extract the bullets. So, while they busied themselves in the kitchen, preparing teas and ointments that would help me heal once the invasive objects were out, Nova ran to another house, where another human wife, Gwen, lived. Gwen was married to a grendel, of course, and she'd come here only a year ago. They were trying for a baby with no luck. I knew it was going to happen for them, but Gwen was so sad about it that she rarely came out of the house anymore. She'd isolated herself, and Nova, Holly, and Maren were worried about her. She hadn't even been to my birthday party a few days ago, so Teal hadn't met her yet.

Gwen was a doctor. Better said, in her previous life, she'd been a doctor. She'd worked at the hospital in her city, until she decided to send her blood to the Temple. That was all I knew about her. She and her husband kept to themselves. Nova was a nurse, but she hadn't practiced in too long, and she didn't think she could help me all by herself. A doctor and a nurse were better than just a nurse.

Gwen came running. She had a first aid kit with her, and as soon as she got to the house, she got to work. Gwen and Nova extracted the bullets one by one, not before pumping me with painkillers, as Gwen put it. Teal never left their side, helping where she could.

I wanted to refuse the painkillers. I was strong. I could take a bit of pain. But when Gwen dug into my flesh to find the first bullet, I had to backtrack and ask for the pills. She gave me an injection instead, saying it would work faster.

It took her until late at night to get all the bullets out and patch my wounds. I was exhausted. I felt sick and vulnerable, and when they tried to give me something to eat, I refused.

"You go eat," I told Teal.

"I ate a bit earlier. I want to stay with you."

"I'm okay." I was dozing off after Gwen had given me another injection. "You take care of yourself." Then I looked over her shoulder, at Nova. "Take care of Teal," I told her.

"Will do. It's a good thing all the bullets are out and you're feeling better, because Teal refused to even wash up, and she barely ate."

"Go," I told Teal again.

She kissed my forehead, and I closed my eyes. All I wanted was to sleep, so my body would heal faster. Sava and Varna had made me drink their special tea, and Gwen had used an ointment they'd made on my wounds. On second thought, it was probably this combination of medicines that was making me feel dead tired.

"I love you," she whispered in my ear.

"I love you, too," I mumbled.

I spent the next two days in bed, recovering. It was embarrassing it was taking me so long to get back on my feet.

Meanwhile, good things were happening, too. Teal had moved into my bedroom, and every night, she slept next to me, curled up against my side. Seeing how I was still in pain, we didn't do anything, but that was all right. In fact, maybe it was better this way. My injuries gave us time to know each other, to sleep next to each other and become so comfortable with each other that we knew no one and nothing was going to tear us apart.

Lust was nice. Love was better.

On the third day, I got out of bed and went into the backyard to watch the sunrise. Teal had woken up briefly and tried to stop me, but I was feeling like a new man. I tucked her back in, kissed her forehead, and told her to sleep for another hour while I fixed breakfast for us.

The eggs were in the pan, frying, and the batter for the pancakes was waiting on the kitchen counter.

There was a knock on the door, and I had to take the eggs off the stove and see who it was.

My brother, Kairos.

He walked in, and I could tell he was agitated.

"What's wrong?" I asked.

"I forgot to tell you! With all that's happened lately, I just forgot. You can't really blame me, can you?"

"Forgot to tell me what?" I was confused. When were we going to have some peace and quiet around here?

"Someone from the Temple is scheduled to arrive later today, before noon, to check up on Teal. The priest said it was the only way he would allow me and Holly to take Teal for you. He is sending a delegate to see how things are going, and hopefully retrieve a copy of the signed marriage contract."

I stared at him with wide eyes, then burst out laughing.

Kairos frowned. "I thought you'd be upset."

"This is great news. Let them come! Before noon, you said? Let's prepare a nice lunch by the river and invite the Temple delegate. I will sign the marriage contract with him present, and whoever else wants to join us. It's better this way. I love the idea! Yes, I want to do this with witnesses."

Kairos relaxed. "Wow, Teal has really changed you, brother."

"Maybe a little."

"For the better."

I laughed. "I agree."

Teal emerged from the bedroom, staring at us. "Agree about what? What's happening?"

"Come, my love. You must be starving."

"What's happening?"

She sat down on the couch, and I went into the kitchen to finish preparing breakfast. Kairos filled her in quickly, then went home to tell Holly. They were tasked with getting everything ready for when the Temple delegate arrived. I knew I could trust them, and I knew Ragnar, Orion, and their wives were going to pitch in. They were over the moon that I was finally going to sign the marriage contract.

It was just a paper. Bureaucracy. Now that I knew I wanted to spend my life with Teal, it was easy to do it. It had been stupid of me to resist this. To fight it. As if one could fight fate...

As she finished eating her breakfast, Teal stood up, alarmed, her mouth still full.

"I have to get ready. I think Nova gave me a white dress. Or should I wear the dress I wore on your birthday?"

"Nothing would make me happier," I said. "Yes, my love, please wear the dress you were wearing when you came out of my birthday cake."

She beamed at me, then ran into our shared bedroom.

The Temple delegate came through the portal. We were waiting for him, Teal and I, hand in hand. He was a middle-aged man dressed in the robes of the Temple, and we invited him to have lunch with us on the river shore.

My family was there, as well as Sava and Varna, who were curious, as always, and didn't want to miss a thing.

Teal looked divine in her white dress. She had a scarf thrown over her shoulders just in case it got chilly later. The weather was ever-changing, as it always was in spring.

We sat down to eat, and for a few minutes, we made light conversation. Then the man started asking Teal questions.

"How have you adapted here?" he asked.

"Just great! I love Mossdale, and I'm happy to call it my home."

"How about your husband? Has he been treating you well?" He shot me a glance, but the question had been directed at Teal, and he made it clear he wanted to hear what she had to say.

Teal chuckled. "I won't lie to you, it was awkward at first. Branthor found out he had a mate when I showed up, out of the blue, and he didn't know how to react. But he's been treating me amazingly. We're really good together."

Out of the blue... More like out of a cake, but I stayed silent.

The man seemed to be satisfied with her answer.

"I brought the marriage contract," I said. "My brother signed it for me, but I know you need my signature to make this marriage truly official."

The man cocked an eyebrow. "You haven't signed it yet?"

I scratched the back of my head, feeling cornered. Teal wrapped herself around my arm, and that soothed me.

"We wanted you to bear witness," she said in a cheerful tone. "Since you were coming anyway, we thought it would be a good idea for him to sign in the presence of a Temple delegate."

Good save. I felt silly, realizing that I couldn't explain myself. I couldn't tell the man that I'd been in doubt about Teal and our life together. How stupid would that have been? I couldn't tell him I'd been ready to take her back to the Temple, regardless of what my own heart had been screaming at me.

The man nodded and accepted Teal's explanation. So, with him bearing witness, I took out a pen and signed the marriage contract.

Teal squealed and wrapped her arms around my neck. She almost slipped and fell, and I caught her and held her gently.

"I got you," I whispered in her ear. "I got you."

She giggled. "I got you, too."

And that made my heart swell with happiness like I'd never felt before.

TEAL

I trembled under the warm touch of my husband. As we stood facing each other in the glow of the fireplace, he undid the zipper of my dress, and it pooled around my ankles. I untucked the hem of his shirt from his pants and undid the few buttons I could reach. He had to unbutton it all the way and remove it, while I struggled with his belt buckle. Undressing a grendel was hard work. Without his help, I didn't think I'd ever be able to remove all his clothes.

Soon enough, we were naked, taking our time looking at each other. It was hard for me to hold his gaze. One, because it was really taxing on my neck, as I constantly needed to crane it, and two... how could I stare into his eyes when I was, in fact, at eye level with his very massive, very erect cock?

This was my chance. I wanted to taste him. I took a step towards him and wrapped both hands around his cock. I moved them up and down, and he growled deep in his chest.

"Teal... what are you doing?"

"What does it look like I'm doing?" I smirked mischievously and gave the tip a lick. "Mm..."

"Don't do that."

He was ready to pull away, but I squeezed his cock hard. Not hard enough to hurt him. As if anything I did could ever hurt him.

"Why not? I want to."

"I don't think I can take it."

"You can," I murmured as I licked at the slit, tasting the translucent beads of precum that had gathered there.

He groaned, and his cock grew harder, the thick veins pulsating underneath my palms. I loved the reactions I elicited from him. His little groans and growls turned me on. With no panties and no bra, my pussy was gushing down my inner thighs, and my nipples were as hard as pebbles. My core throbbed with lust. I wanted him inside me, but I wanted to drink what he was willing to give me, too.

Though, if he came... Remembering how hard he'd come inside me, and how much seed he'd pumped into my pussy... I didn't think I could swallow even a quarter of it. An idea came to me. What if...

"I want you to come on my body," I said, my heart fluttering in my chest, my stomach tight.

He looked down at me, puzzled. "I don't know, Teal. I'm not sure."

"I am." I stroked his cock again, running my hands up and down the length, using his precum and my saliva to give him a two-hand job. He groaned long and deep. "I'll take that as a yes."

He shook his head but didn't contradict me. I went back to work.

It was a good thing that, at least, from my height, I could reach his cock. Giving a blowjob while standing was surprisingly comfortable. I couldn't suck the head of his cock into my mouth – it was that big – but I could lick it and nip at it, suck the very tip, where more precum seeped through the slit. I saw him curl his hands into fists at his sides. I wanted to see his face as I licked and stroked his massive cock, but that meant pulling away and craning my neck upwards. I rather liked what I was doing and didn't want to stop.

"Teal... I'm close," he said. "You have to stop now."

"Mm... no..."

He grabbed me by the shoulders, and I yelped when he pushed me away then scooped me into his arms and carried me to the bed. My yelp turned into laughter.

"Seriously? I wasn't even doing much," I said.

"Oh, you were doing plenty."

When he lay me down and climbed on top of me, pushing my legs apart, I whined.

"But I want you to come on my body."

"Soon," he said. "I need to be inside you now."

He used the oil that was always on the nightstand, within reach, and poured some into his hand. He rubbed his hands together, then proceeded to lather the oil all over my pussy and inner thighs. He slipped one finger inside me, and I arched my back and moaned. I placed my hands on his shoulders, my nails digging into his skin.

"You're so beautiful," he whispered. "I want to make you come."

"Mm..." I bit my lip.

"How many times do you want to come, Teal?"

I chuckled. "Not too many. Last time, I almost passed out."

"Last time was your first time. You're not a virgin anymore, you can take a few orgasms."

"I don't think that's how it works." Once wasn't nearly enough to get used to Branthor. My pussy was still inexperienced.

He ignored me and moved down my body to flick my clit with the tip of his tongue. Between that and his finger pumping in and out of me, the first orgasm hit me like an ocean wave. I let out a cry and arched into him, my hands going to his head, pressing him down, where I needed him most. He sucked my clit into his mouth, then my folds, cleaning me thoroughly. A second finger joined the first, and he scissored them slowly, stretching me for what would come next.

"Just... take me now..." I panted. "I want your cock, not your fingers."

He looked up at me, and our eyes met. His were deep green and filled with lust.

"Say that again."

"Why?" I giggled.

"I love hearing you beg for my cock."

"Will you come all over me after you fuck me?"

"Promise."

"Then... I want your cock inside me, husband."

He growled and removed his fingers, quickly positioning the head of his cock at my entrance. I felt my pussy literally opening and stretching for him, inviting him in. I was eager to feel the fulness that only he could give me. He slipped inside me one inch at a time, and thanks to the oil, I didn't feel any pain. It was all pure pleasure and the feeling of being filled. Branthor was careful, but not afraid. The first time we'd had sex, he'd been terrified he might hurt me. Now he knew I didn't break easily.

"You're so tight, wife," he murmured.

I couldn't help a giggle. That was right, we were married. Earlier today, he'd signed the marriage contract, at last, and the delegate from the Temple had left satisfied, with a copy. It was official. I was his, he was mine, and he couldn't back down now. Not even if he did get a little scared sometimes.

"Only for you," I said.

He thrust inside me all the way, letting out a groan and leaning in to kiss me. The kiss was long and passionate. He teased me and explored my mouth, waiting for me to adapt to his length and girth. Not once did he let his weight push me into the mattress. He made sure to brace himself on his knees and elbows, hovering over me at all times. I bucked my hips into his, and he knew I was done waiting. I wanted him to move.

He pulled out slowly, then pushed back in. My legs clung to his waist, my heels digging into the back of his thighs. He was so wide that I couldn't hook my ankles around him, but I could urge him to move faster in other ways. I pulled at his hair and forced him to look into my eyes.

"Fuck me like you mean it," I said.

In response, he licked his lips and thrust harder inside me. "The things you do to me…"

I held on to him as his thrusts became more erratic, as if he could barely hold himself back. I didn't want him to, but I knew that if he didn't practice patience and control, he could easily crush me. One wrong move, one thrust that was too deep or too hard, and what we were doing could've ended in something else than an orgasm. Better not to go there.

There was no point to my dark thoughts anyway, because Branthor was the most gentle and attentive lover. He paid attention to the sounds I made, to the expression on my face, and to the way my body moved under him.

His cock reached deep inside me. So deep that I was confused about the anatomy of my own body. The mushroom head hit my cervix over and over again, and thanks to the oil, all I felt was bliss. My eyes rolled in my head as I came, harder than before. It was nice when he got me off with his mouth and fingers, but his cock was entirely different. It could make my soul leave my body for a second, and when it rushed back in, I felt like a different woman.

He pulled out of me just as I was starting to come down from the orgasm. At first, I didn't understand what was happening. I sat up to look at him, my legs shaking as he removed them from around his waist. He was on his knees, still between my legs, and his hand was around his cock. My eyes widened at the sight of Branthor masturbating.

It only took a few pumps, hard and frenzied, and he was coming in spurts, all over my chest, stomach, and legs. His cum was thick and white, slightly transparent, and it was almost hot as it hit my skin. My breasts were bathed in it. It trickled down my stomach, making its way between my legs. Eager to have it inside me, I threw all shame out the window and started touching myself. With my fingers, I started pushing his seed between my folds, rubbing my clit with it, then inside my pussy. My fingers came out for more, and Branthor gave me more. It was as if he couldn't stop coming.

The sheets were a mess. I wasn't sure we could wash them. Easier to throw them away and get new ones. But if we were going to do this a few times a week...

"Do that again?" he said, out of breath. "Show me how you pleasure yourself."

I blushed. Truth be told, I hadn't touched myself before this. What I was doing was instinctive, not learned. It felt right, so I put on a show for him. I leaned back against the pillows and started running my other hand over my breasts. I spread his cum thoroughly all over my body. With the other hand, I kept directing it inside my pussy, fingering myself, going deeper and deeper, curling my fingers to hit the spot that made me breathe faster.

"Yes," he said. "Make yourself come. Come for me, Teal."

He kept stroking his cock. He positioned himself in such a way that the next string of cum hit my clit. I let out a moan and came right then and there. I felt my pussy gushing, and I arched my back, fingering myself to completion. Branthor let go of his cock and leaned over me, his hand covering mine on my pussy.

"You're so good," he said as he captured my lips in a kiss. "You're so good to me, Teal."

"Of course I am." I found that I could barely speak. I was spent. "I'm your wife. The wife you didn't want."

He groaned. "I wanted you from the first minute I saw you. I just didn't want to admit it to myself."

"Good thing I'm stubborn, too."

"More stubborn than me, possibly."

"I think so. Aren't you glad?"

"So glad."

He laughed, letting his heavy body crash beside me. I climbed on top of him and curled up on his chest, like a cat. A very wet, very dirty cat.

"We should shower," I said.

"Later."

He wrapped his arms around me and held me gently. His chest rose and fell, lulling me to sleep.

Later sounded just perfect.

Epilogue
Branthor

Six Months Later

It was a different feeling, a novel way of life... To know what my purpose was. I looked at my wife's pretty face, at her white-blonde hair tucked in a loose ponytail, at her long neck, now heavy breasts, and round belly carrying life within... And I was shocked I could feel so much joy and fulfillment, and not burst at the seams.

Before Teal came into my life, I'd been drifting, and I hadn't even known it. Watching my brothers with their families, thinking I could never do what they did. It was too much dedication, too much work. And oh, how wrong had I been! In fact, it was all love, devotion, and happiness. Teal had taught me all of it, and to thank her for the greatest lesson I'd ever learned, I was going to serve her for as long as I lived.

She was in the living room, trying to knit a baby jumper. "Trying" being the keyword. Holly had taken up knitting when her daughter was born, and she swore by it as a means of relaxation. Lately, Teal had felt stressed because of the pregnancy, and Holly had taught her how to knit. It wasn't going great, but my wife was determined. I watched her from the kitchen, where three different dishes were cooking at the same time, one in the oven and two on the stove. She was making progress in the knitting department, but not in the relaxation department. If anything, the whole process seemed to cause her frustration.

The first three months were always the hardest. Holly, Nova, and Maren had all confirmed it. Especially since this was our first baby, Teal went through terrible symptoms that started in the morning. She hadn't eaten at all today. Only drank some water, apple juice, and ate some fruits. The sickness only subsided in the evening, but even then, she was fussy when it came to food. Hence the three different dishes.

I was happy to cook her four, five, six dishes! Only to see her eat.

All she had to do was exist and find ways to lower her stress. If knitting wasn't going to work out, I was thinking of suggesting painting or writing. We took long walks every day. Just like me, she loved the Thundering Caves. I never let her explore them without me.

In fact, I rarely let her do anything on her own. It wasn't because she needed me, but because I needed her. I wanted to spend every waking moment with her. After six months of being together, I couldn't understand how I'd lived without her before.

She dropped the needles in the knitting basket, crossed her arms over her chest, and glared at them.

"I hate this," she said.

I did my best to stifle a chuckle. It wasn't a good idea to laugh at her expense when she was feeling so frustrated.

"I don't know how Holly does it. Does our baby even need a jumper?"

"Whatever our baby needs, I will provide," I said from the kitchen.

She looked up at me and sniffed the air. "Smells good."

"Great! Because you need to eat."

"I'm hungry, believe me." She sighed as she stood up and came to join me. "But more often than not, I just throw up whatever I eat, and it's exhausting."

"I know, my love. I know." I kissed the top of her head as I stirred the vegetable stew. Lately, she hadn't been that much into meat.

"And I'm sweating! Why am I sweating so much?"

"Do you want to go out on the porch? Dinner will be ready in ten minutes. It's hot in here, you don't have to stay with me."

"Aww..." She clung to my arm. "But I want to. I love watching you cook. You're so sexy."

I laughed. "Yes, that's why I'm doing it. I just want to look hot, so you'd get naked with me later."

She punched me lightly. "You're a tease."

I grinned at her. She went outside, though. There were beads of sweat along her hairline, and she needed some air. Unfortunately, this was the greatest disadvantage of a human female carrying a half-grendel baby. The pregnancy was hard. It made me reconsider the number of children I wanted. It was entirely up to Teal, anyway. I had no say in it.

The backyard was all lit up. It was a peaceful evening, and the sun had just dipped beneath the horizon. The moon, surrounded by bright stars, took command of the sky. The air was fresh, smelling of pine and the myriad of flowers that grew in our garden. I carried our dinner to the table on the porch, and Teal watched me with a bright smile on her face.

"What?" I asked as I sat down.

"Nothing."

I cocked an eyebrow at her. "No, what?"

She shrugged. "I was just thinking... How things have changed. How different my life is, and how I'd never thought I'd be the one to sit back as someone else did everything for me."

She'd told me about her family. About her mother, who'd died before she turned eighteen and told her to send her blood to the Temple. About her father and two brothers, who'd taken advantage of her and basically turned her into a maid. I couldn't help feeling like it was my fault. Had I gotten over myself five years ago and sent my blood to the Temple, Teal and I would've been matched, and she never would've had to endure the abuse of the men in her family.

Of course, I couldn't turn back time. All I could do was thank my brothers for tricking me, stealing my blood, and making Teal hide in my birthday cake. I had the rest of my life to make it up to her for how much of an idiot I'd been.

"Better get used to it," I said. "This is your new normal."

She laughed as she surveyed the food, trying to decide what she wanted.

"Got used to it already. But, just saying... I appreciate it."

"And I appreciate you."

I reached over the table and took her hand in mine, then bent down to kiss it. She blushed cutely, like she always did. The sight of her rosy cheeks was all I needed to know that I was finally fulfilling my purpose.

This was right. My only job was to be a great husband to Teal, and a great father to our baby. I could do it, and more than that...

It was an honor.

Arranged Monster Mates

Wed to the Ice Giant, by Layla Fae
Wed to the Minotaur, by Eden Ember
Wed to the Wolfman, by Cara Wylde
Wed to the Phoenix, by Eden Ember
Wed to the Dragon, by Cara Wylde
Wed to the Orc, by Layla Fae
Wed to the Lionman, by Cara Wylde
Wed to the Lich, by Layla Fae
Wed to the Bullman, by Eden Ember
Wed to Jack Frost, by Layla Fae
Wed to the Dark Elf, by Eden Ember
Wed to Krampus, by Cara Wylde
Wed to the Gargoyle, by Eden Ember
Wed to the Basilisk, by Layla Fae

Orc Mates

Vorgak the Cruel
Rogan the Gray
Kaius the Fierce
Baruk the Cursed
Grimor the Joyless
Torgar the Molten
Uthar the Hunter
Toghat the Vile
Kelraz the Vicious

Printed in Dunstable, United Kingdom